The Diary and the Green Dress

By

Shelley Banks

Chapter One

It was unlike any dress she'd ever seen—mint green, drop-waisted, three-quarter length, with beading along the neckline, sleeves and hem. The material was exquisite; shimmery, soft, and silky to touch. Fragile though. It would need to be covered and hung up when she had the chance. It couldn't stay in the dust-covered trunk where she'd found it. It was too beautiful to be hidden away. Next to the trunk was a timber chair and desk. It was a small desk, with one drawer. Every other room in the house was empty.

The search for the house had been long and frustrating. Each Saturday, for five months, Izzy had gone to open homes, and she'd become very good at translating the selling points. "Great location close to transport" meant a busy main road with a popular bus stop out the front. "Needs some TLC" indicated that no one had looked after the place in thirty years. "City views" meant either of two things; if there was a good view of the city, the price went up by $200,000 and was out of her price range. Or, there was a glimpse of a high-rise above the treetops. Which apparently was enough to be classed as a city view. So when she first stood outside this particular house, it had been hard to contain her excitement. She'd seen pictures on the internet, but the first few were dreadful, so she'd skipped the rest. But a few weeks later, it was still being advertised, so she'd decided to drive by and have a look from the outside. When she got home, she rang and made an appointment to inspect the property.

From the moment she walked in, she knew it was the one. Built in 1919, the house had features that she loved. VJ walls. Ten-foot-high ceilings made of pressed tin with ceiling roses in the centre where vintage pendant lights dangled on chains and cords. There were casement windows, some with stained glass panels. And wide timber floorboards, which would have had many unknown feet tread across them.

The house needed some work, but it was only cosmetic—some new curtains, a fresh coat of off-white paint on the walls, a few thick rugs on the floor. As she walked from room to room, she started picturing where she would put her furniture, as if this was already her home. Not that she told the real estate agent that. He was pushy enough as it was, and she wasn't going to hurry. It was too big a decision. Instead, she walked out to the wide, shaded verandah that wrapped around three sides of the house and stood for a few minutes. The breeze felt lovely against her skin, and the view over the surrounding hilly suburbs, with their mix of old and new houses almost hidden by trees, was something she could quickly get used to looking at each day. She could hear the real estate agent moving around inside, eager for her to finish the tour and find out if she was interested. And if not, to hurry up and go so he could move on to the next potential buyer, the ever-present promise of a commission at the front of his mind. Izzy wasn't ready to go back in and talk to him, so she walked down the back stairs and into the yard. It was small, but she didn't need anything bigger. And the gardens were well established if a bit overgrown. Some time and some weeding would take care of that. Maybe a few plants with colourful flowers in amongst all the greenery would liven the garden up. As with inside, she started picturing what the garden would look like as if it was already hers.

After a few more minutes wandering around the yard and looking up at the outside of the house, which was painted in the traditional colours of classic cream, manor red and cottage green instead of the pale grey now popular across the Brisbane landscape, she went back inside. Izzy told the agent she was interested but wanted to come back on the weekend for another inspection to see what the area was like when everyone was home. She also wanted a second opinion.

"Morning."

Izzy turned around at the sound of the loud, cheerful voice and smiled as she watched Teresa walk towards her in her usual weekend outfit of shorts and a t-shirt. Teresa had never been one to dress up if she didn't have to. Not to say she didn't do a fantastic job when she did. The fact that she could afford perfectly tailored outfits, as opposed to the ones Izzy bought off the rack, helped. Izzy had never seen her in a dress that didn't do justice to her slim figure, jet black hair, blue eyes and pale skin that she slathered with SPF50 sunscreen every time she ventured outside. An Irish ancestor somewhere in her family heritage was responsible for the genetic make-up that was unsuited to Australia's unforgiving summers.

"I wasn't sure which house it was," she said as they hugged. "It's hard to see the house numbers through all the trees."

The trees were something that attracted Izzy in the first place. They gave the street a calm, comforting feeling. After the past few years, living in a street like this was exactly what she needed.

"So, are we going in?" Teresa asked. Izzy looked at the grin on Teresa's face. "I think you're more excited than I am at the moment."

"I doubt that. But I am excited for you."

Izzy opened the gate. She could see the real estate agent standing on the verandah, peering down at them with an impatient look on his face.

"You'd think he'd be happier considering you've come back for a second look," Teresa said.

"I'm sure he'll be happier if I decide to buy it."

As she walked through the house with Teresa, looking in the rooms and imagining again what they would look like with her furniture, she found it hard to keep a smile off her face. After they'd finished the tour of the house, they walked out to the yard so they could talk without being overheard.

Izzy turned to Teresa. "What do you think?"

"It's fantastic. I love it."

"You're not just saying that?"

"Of course not. I'm your best friend. I would never lie about something so important. It's so exciting to think this could soon be yours."

"And scary too. I've never owned a house before."

Teresa put her arm around Izzy. "Nothing to be scared about. The mortgage repayments will be about the same as what you're paying in rent, and you easily manage that every week."

Teresa was right. Izzy had always been a good budgeter and never had any problems paying her bills or saving money. Probably a handy trait to have, seeing as she was an accountant, she thought to herself. She turned and looked at the house again. It was everything she wanted, so she took a deep breath, went back to the agent and said she wanted to make an offer.

Izzy sighed as she looked at all the things she'd have to pack if things worked out. She'd need to have a cleanout first. She wasn't even sure why she kept half the things she had, especially the gifts from Jason. They should have been thrown out two years ago. In her pocket, her phone started ringing.

"Any news yet?" her mum Julia asked.

The negotiations had been going on for three weeks. Every time Izzy put in an offer, another one came back from the seller asking for more.

"Not yet. If my latest offer isn't accepted, I'll have to let the house go. I can't afford to pay any more."

"Fingers crossed. Either way, I'm sure you'll hear something soon."

"I just don't know why they advertised a price that was clearly lower than what they wanted for the house."

"Because they're trying to get as much money as they can. I know how much you love the house, but there's no point putting yourself under financial stress for it. If the house is meant to be yours, then it will be."

Her mum had been right. She usually was. The agent rang late that afternoon to say the house was hers. After she hung up, she sat on her lounge chair and didn't move. But she smiled and couldn't stop. Eventually, she got up, went to the fridge, opened the champagne she'd bought in the hope that this moment would happen and said a toast. For the moment, all thoughts of how much packing she'd have to do were gone. Instead, her thoughts were consumed by her house, the first one she'd bought by herself.

"Are you sad to leave?" Julia asked four weeks later.

Izzy looked around the house that had been her home for the past two years and shook her head. Too many days with too many tears, at least in the first few months. After that, things had been better. But in the beginning, it was hard. Especially that first day, as she sat on the floor with boxes all around her, wondering how her life had changed so dramatically in such a short time.

Izzy's dad Ben walked over to where they were standing. "The last box is in the car. Just some pieces of furniture left to go on the truck."

Julia looked out the window towards the truck parked on the driveway. "What are those removalists doing?"

"Probably not much," Izzy muttered.

When the removalists first arrived, she'd taken them through each room and showed them what needed to go into the truck. They seemed eager to get on with it, so she left them to it. Thirty minutes later, she looked out the window and saw them in the front yard, sitting on her lounge chair eating sandwiches. They'd carried it out the door then sat down for a break. A few politely spoken but firm words were exchanged, and they'd started again. Apparently, not for long. It didn't look like anything was happening out there.

"I'll go and check," Ben said.

Izzy didn't know what he said to them, but within two minutes, they were back inside, picking up her dining room table. She was about to thank him and her mum for all the help when she heard Teresa's voice.

"Hello. Where are you?"

"In the kitchen."

"I'm just on my way to drop Jack and Rosie off for a play date and saw your car out front. How's it all going?"

"We're almost done."

"That's because you had helpers," Ben said as he walked into the room.

Izzy hugged him. "And I appreciate it."

     <u>The Diary and the Green Dress</u>

"We know. How are you, Teresa?"

"Good thanks, Ben. Is Julia here too?"

Izzy's mum heard her name and joined them in the kitchen.

"Here I am."

Teresa looked around. "I had to have one last look before you left. We had some good nights here."

"We did," Izzy said.

Eventually, she thought to herself, remembering those nights when Teresa had comforted her in the months after she'd moved in. But she brushed those thoughts aside. This was a time for looking forward, not looking back. Today was the day she was moving into her own house—a house where no one could do anything that would make her leave. Or take the life she thought was hers away from her.

Even though Teresa didn't stay long, Izzy was glad she'd called in. She'd been there for the beginning, and she was there for the end. The visit was long enough, though, for Jack and Rosie to ask Izzy if she'd already packed the chocolate biscuits she usually had in the pantry. Their looks of disappointment when she said she had, made them all laugh. Izzy promised to have some ready when they came to visit her at the new house. As she watched them go, she wondered what she would have done without Teresa.

When everything was complete, Izzy shut the front door and walked to her car, stopping only to take one last look at what had been her home for the past two years. She'd already said goodbye to the neighbours. There was nothing else to do but reverse out of the driveway and head towards her new life.

An hour and a half later, Izzy shut the front gate as she watched the removalists drive away. They'd done a much quicker job unloading her furniture, which probably had something to do with Izzy hearing one of them say they were off to the pub as soon as they were done. She had just started walking up the front stairs when she heard a voice.

"Hello. You must be my new neighbour. I'm Harry."

"Hello, Harry. I'm Izzy, short for Isabel."

"Welcome to the neighbourhood Izzy. It's a lovely area. I'm sure you'll enjoy living here."

"I'm sure I will. How long have you lived in this street?"

"I've been here since 1959. Moved in just after I got married."

"You must have seen a lot of changes."

"Yes, there's been a fair bit of change in the area over the years. And changes to your house too. I'll tell you about them over a cuppa one day. I'm sure you've got a lot to do, and I need to continue my walk. I go for an hour every day. Not bad for eighty-three. I'll see you later."

Izzy watched as Harry continued his walk. It would be interesting to hear what he had to say about the history of the area. And her house.

Back inside, she started to unpack and had just finished hanging up her clothes in the wardrobe when she heard a knock on the door.

"I couldn't wait to see it again," Teresa said. "And I thought you could use a hand unpacking."

"You don't have to do that."

"I know, but I want to, and I don't need to pick up Jack and Rosie for another hour. But you have to show me around again first. I've forgotten what the rooms look like."

A quick tour followed, and it ended in the only room Izzy hadn't shown Teresa last time because the agent had been in there talking on the phone. The room with the trunk, desk and chair.

"This is my favourite room in the house. It's only small, but it feels cosy, and there's just something about it. Almost like I can tell that someone spent a lot of time in this room, and they were happy in here."

Teresa raised her eyebrows.

"I know it sounds crazy, but every time I walk in, I get that feeling."

"This is an old house. I'm sure lots of different people have lived here over the years. Someone would have loved this room."

"I guess so."

Teresa pointed to the trunk. "I haven't seen that before. Or that chair and desk. Did you buy them?"

Izzy shook her head. "They're not mine. They were left here after the previous owner's possessions were moved."

"Can you return them?"

Izzy shook her head. "I bought the house from a deceased estate—a woman named Hettie Barclay—and the solicitor said there were no surviving relatives."

"Have you looked inside the trunk?"

Izzy nodded.

"I don't suppose it's filled with treasure."

"No, but it does contain something beautiful."

"Can I see?"

"Of course. Open the lid."

Teresa held up the mint green dress with the beautiful beading and lacework. "It's exquisite."

Izzy nodded. "I'll hang it up in my wardrobe when I've sorted that out. I wonder who it belonged to?"

"It looks old. The 1920s, maybe?"

"The style is right for that era."

"Is there anything else in the trunk?"

"There's a beaded headband and a small clutch purse. They belong with the dress."

Teresa pulled them out of the trunk. The clutch purse was made from the same mint green material and had matching beads that ran in a line across the top, just below the clasp. The headband, also covered in the same material, had beads running through the centre from one side to the other.

"Is that a blanket?" Teresa asked, peering back into the trunk.

Izzy nodded. "I haven't taken it out yet. The dress is much more interesting."

Teresa looked again. "I think there's something under the blanket."

Izzy watched as she pulled out fifteen leather-bound diaries. They all had brown covers, closer to tan than dark brown, with unlined cream paper inside. Each one looked to be what, in paper terms, would be called A5. And the ones they opened were filled with small, neat handwriting in black ink.

"There's an envelope too with a name on the front. Someone called Grace."

"Let's open it and see what's in there."

Out of the envelope came a bundle of letters and some photos which were stuck together.

The first letter was dated in the 1920s. Unfortunately, the last number was faded, so they couldn't make out the exact year. The paper was thin and unlined, and the words, like those in the diaries, were written in black ink.

"Listen to this," Izzy said.

Dear Grace

As I sat down to write this letter, I knew that giving it to you would be the last time I would see you. The thought of not having you in my life is almost too hard to bear but what I'm doing is for the best. I've taken a job in Melbourne. When I told your Father, he thought it would be perfect for my future prospects. I had agreed because I didn't want to tell him the real reason—that I love you, but we can never be together. The time I've

    <u>The Diary and the Green Dress</u>

spent with you has been the happiest of my life. Take care of yourself and Hettie. I will think of you both every day. I love you.

Yours always, Bryce.

"What a beautiful letter," Izzy said. "I wonder who Grace and Bryce were?"

"No idea, but the Hettie mentioned must be the one who owned this house. When you have time, you should go through the letters and diaries and see what you can find. Right now, we need to unpack. I'll have to go soon."

Before she left, Teresa asked Izzy what she was doing the following Sunday.

"No plans. Why?"

"I'm having a BBQ. Do you want to come over?"

"Sure, sounds good."

"Great, I'll see you then. Love the house."

After Teresa had gone, Izzy's thoughts turned back to Grace and Bryce. Who were they? And what had happened between them that caused Bryce to write such a letter?

The next day, after many hours spent unpacking, Izzy sat on the verandah with a coffee and the diaries. The rest of the letters were fragile, having been written on the same thin paper as the first, so she'd decided to leave them for the moment. The fifteen diaries covered the years between 1919 and 1969, with some entries being each day and others being weeks apart. She picked up the first diary and started to read.

6 January 1919

Mother and Father invited Martin to join us for lunch today. It's the first time I've seen him since he came back. Most people refer to men like Martin as having come back from overseas where they did their duty for King and Country. But to me, he went to war. I don't know much about this war or wars in general, but I don't think it was the great adventure that everyone spoke about in 1914. A great adventure - is that what men said to convince themselves to go? Is that what women told themselves so they didn't have to think that they might never see their husbands or sons again? I've seen the women in town wearing black. There are a lot of them for a city the size of ours, although Brisbane seems to be getting bigger by the month. Martin was polite and spoke to us when he needed to, but he wasn't as talkative as he used to be. There was a brief conversation about Martin coming to work for Father, but nothing was confirmed. Nor was anything said about me at lunch or as he was leaving. Ever since we were young, there has been an understanding that Martin and I would get married one day. Maybe he's changed his mind.

Izzy had never met anyone who'd come back from a war. Her great-grandfather had fought in World War I like the Martin she was reading about. He'd lied about his age to enlist. She'd seen a photo and her mum still had his medals, but she didn't know much about him. She knew a bit more about her grandfather on her dad's side, who had fought in World War II and had died before Izzy was born. Her dad had been a later-in-life surprise for his parents, so he didn't know what his dad was like before the war. But as a child, he remembered his dad coming home from work each day reeking of beer. She continued to read, but it was several pages before she found the next mention of Martin.

2 March 1919

Martin called around to the house two days ago. Father continues to talk to him about joining the business. He told me he was doing that because he and Martin had discussed the future and whether it was still Martin's intention to marry me. Father said it was, but Martin hasn't asked me yet. I'm not sure how I would feel if Martin has changed his mind. Part of me would be sad because I've become used to the idea that this is my future, but part of me would be happy because maybe I could decide what my future will be. There seem to be very few options for women. The world has changed so much over the past few years, and while the war was on, women took on roles they couldn't before. Now it's over, and the men have come home, it seems women have to go back to their houses and stay there. I don't want to spend my life like that. There must be something more. If I

    <u>The Diary and the Green Dress</u>

had any sort of choice, what could I do? I shouldn't think that way, though. I know there are no choices for me.

Izzy put down the diary and felt sad for a person she'd never met. And then she felt sorrow for a marriage she thought would be in her own future. But what she thought and what happened were two different things.

Chapter Two

Izzy looked at her watch and put down the shears. She'd spent a satisfying morning pulling out weeds and pruning trees, but the BBQ at Teresa's was starting in an hour, and she couldn't go dressed in her yard clothes. As she headed inside, she took one more look around the yard and said a silent thank you to Hettie Barclay because she must have had a green thumb. It had only taken a couple of hours to reveal how much time and effort had gone into creating the garden. Now Izzy had an oasis in her backyard full of lush green plants, all different but all hardy varieties. Each one was planted with an even amount of space between it and the next one. She'd uncovered two small garden statues: female figurines, one holding a flowerpot and the other holding a birdbath. Through the middle, she'd found round, smoothed down stones which, when she'd finished unearthing the garden from under the weeds, she realised they joined together to make a path from one end to the other. As she looked around her, she wondered if there had once been a seat among the plants where Hettie had sat and admired her work. It was something she'd never know, but the hours she'd spent in the garden had left her wanting to find out more about its creator.

"You made it," Teresa said. "I wasn't sure if you could tear yourself away from your new house."

"It was hard to leave," Izzy replied with a smile. "But I said I'd come, so here I am."

"Let's go outside and join the others."

Teresa had set up a long timber table under the arbour next to the pool. She had placed blue and white cushions on the two long bench seats that sat on either side, the colours of the cushions matching the tablecloth and napkins. Along the middle of the table, she'd placed flower arrangements that continued the colour theme by featuring blue as well as white geraniums. The plates, white in the middle surrounded by a blue infinity design around the outside, were another nod to the Greek theme Teresa had decided on, as would be the food when it was served. When Teresa hosted a BBQ, it was never just sausages and a garden salad, so today, they were having lamb chops, chicken kebabs, and pork koftas served with Greek salad and grilled halloumi. With Christmas just a week and a half away, Izzy asked her why she hadn't gone with a festive season themed BBQ.

"Too obvious," she said, smiling.

As Izzy looked around, she counted twelve people standing around the table, three she didn't know, including a work colleague of Teresa's named Trent.

"How do you know Teresa?" Trent asked after they were introduced.

"We met at university when we were both standing in line one day at the cafeteria. There was only one ham and salad roll left, and we both wanted it. So we started talking, and we've been friends ever since."

Trent laughed. "That's a good story."

"How long have you known Teresa?"

"I started working at the same company eight months ago. It didn't take me long to realise that she's always looking out for everyone."

Izzy nodded. "That's Teresa. What do you do?"

"I manage the IT department."

"So, you're the person that gets called when something goes wrong with a computer."

"That's me. Also, when phones aren't doing what they should. Or the tablets or the AV system in the office. It's a long list."

"I'm sure you're a very popular person."

They continued talking, and when it came time for lunch, they sat next to each other. After the food had been eaten and the plates cleared away, Izzy realised that she'd hardly spoken to anyone else since she'd been introduced to Trent. And then he asked if she'd been planning on coming with someone. Izzy paused for a moment, then shook her head.

"Me either. I almost didn't come, but Teresa can be very persuasive."

"Yes, she can be. I almost didn't come either. I just bought a house, and I've still got some unpacking to do."

"Congratulations. Where did you buy?"

"At Windsor."

"That's a nice area. My grandfather grew up there."

"I like it. It's close to the city, but my street is quiet. There's a park nearby, and public transport is handy. There are some great coffee shops as well."

Izzy knew she was prattling, but she couldn't help it.

"I don't do much in the mornings until I've had my coffee," Trent said.

"Me either."

"Maybe we could catch up sometime for a coffee."

Izzy hesitated before replying, the end of her last relationship still painfully fresh in her mind. Also in her mind was Teresa. She'd been on at Izzy for months about dating again, and she'd never hear the end of it if she didn't at least have coffee with him. It would just be a coffee, after all.

"Ok. That would be nice."

"How about next Sunday morning? 10 am? We could have brunch rather than just coffee."

Izzy nodded. Maybe she shouldn't have said yes. Coffee was something that could be over quickly if things weren't going well. Brunch would go for much longer.

"We can meet at one of the coffee shops near you."

Izzy picked the first one that came to mind. After he'd gone, she thought of several nicer places she could have chosen. As she went to pick up her bag and leave, she could see Teresa looking at her and smiling.

A week later, Izzy stood in front of her wardrobe and discovered she had nothing to wear. Twenty minutes spent staring at her clothes had brought her no closer to changing out of her pyjamas and into something else. The only thing she'd pulled out was the mint green dress which she'd finally hung up in her wardrobe with a transparent cover over it for protection. She sighed and picked up the phone.

"Teresa, why am I doing this?"

"Because he's a nice guy, and it wouldn't hurt you to go on a date. It's been long enough."

"Well, I can't go. I've got nothing to wear."

"You have plenty to wear. How about that jade green and cream sleeveless dress you wore to lunch the other week?"

Izzy had to admit that the dress did highlight her shoulder-length light auburn hair and hazel eyes. It even set off the tan she'd acquired on a recent weekend at the beach. She'd always tanned easily. Even though laying in the sun was something she'd done when she was younger, all the warnings about skin cancer had stopped her doing that years ago. Still, it only took two mornings of swimming in the ocean for her skin to tan.

"I suppose I could wear that. But, I'm still not sure I should go."

"Why? What's the worst that can happen? You run out of things to talk about, and you come home early."

"I'm more worried that we'll have plenty to talk about, and he'll ask me out again."

"Isn't that the point?"

"I don't know if I'm ready for that."

"Of course you are. What happened last time was awful, but it's time to get back out there."

The last time, Izzy thought to herself after she hung up. The relationship she thought she'd been in for life. Jason told her he felt the same. Except that he was sleeping around behind her back. Izzy sat down on the bed and reached for a tissue, then turned to look at the clock. Too late to cancel now. She got up, went into the bathroom, splashed cold water on her face and put on the dress. She debated whether to put make-up on before deciding on just a light foundation and a clear lip gloss. It was Sunday morning at a café, after all, not Saturday night in a club.

Trent was already seated when she got there but stood up when he saw her. On the way there, she'd been thinking about what he looked like, wondering if she remembered correctly his light brown hair, brown eyes and the fact that he was taller than her, even though she'd been wearing her wedge heels. And the way his smile lit up his face. Slow down, she told herself. Don't let your guard down just because he's good looking and clearly spends some of his time at the gym.

"I got here early to make sure we got a table. I'll get us a coffee, and then we can look at the menu if you like."

Izzy sat down as he went to the counter. Was she ready if something came from this?

"Coffee will be here in a minute," Trent said when he came back. "How was your week?"

"It was busy. Work has been hectic, and I'm still unpacking the last of the boxes. You only realise how much stuff you have when you move."

Trent nodded. "I bought a house in Alderley eighteen months ago. It took a long time to pack, and I threw out a lot of things I forgot I had. I'm sure if I went through everything again, I'd find more to get rid of."

"There were a lot of things I forgot I had too."

And a lot she should have thrown out two years ago, she reminded herself but didn't say aloud.

"So, when you're not unpacking, what do you like to do?"

"I like gardening. I get a sense of achievement in seeing something I've planted grow."

"I tend to kill any plant I come in contact with. Golf is my hobby."

      The Diary and the Green Dress

"How long have you been playing?"

"Eleven years. I play in a competition on Saturday mornings."

"I've never played before. I keep thinking it's something I should try, but I've never got around to it."

They sat and talked for the next two hours, and Izzy was surprised how quickly the time went. And how much she'd enjoyed herself. This was why she agreed to Trent introducing her to golf the weekend after Christmas. She watched as he drove off and then started walking home. Not long after she walked in the door, the phone rang.

"Have you got spies outside telling you I just got home?"

Teresa laughed. "Just good timing. So…?"

"We're seeing each other the first weekend after Christmas."

"That's fantastic."

"I'm still not sure I'm doing the right thing."

"Yes, you are. Stop thinking about it and just go for it."

Izzy spent the rest of the day in the garden, the cool, rich soil and leafy plants calming her thoughts. She hoped Teresa was right. When Izzy had finished, she looked at what she'd accomplished. The last remaining weeds were gone. She'd planted some Agapanthus, Begonia, Hibiscus, Frangipani and Bougainvillea among the greenery, all chosen for their vibrant, intense colours that would continue to shine, even if the day came that the sunlight was taken away.

That night, though she was tired, she wanted to know more about Grace, Martin and, after another day in her garden, maybe something about Hettie. If she'd been mentioned in the letter, then chances were she'd be mentioned in the diaries. The first two entries had grabbed her interest straight away, so instead of going to sleep as she should have, she picked up the first diary, turned to the second page and settled in on her lounge chair. As soon as she saw the word proposal, Izzy wondered whether she should skip the entry, her memories telling her it was not something she should be reading about. But she decided to anyway. It was someone else's life, she told herself.

Martin proposed today. It was very formal. I'd always imagined that when a proposal came, it would be romantic. But I said yes, and plans are starting to be made. Soon, I'll no longer be Grace Andrews. I'll be Grace Barclay. First, I shall have to start sewing my dress. Mother said she would help me. I could get a seamstress to do it, but I'd like to do it myself. It will mean more to me that way, and I'll be able to have more say in what the dress looks like. I'm sure Mother will have very definite views, but hopefully, I'll have some influence. And if not, I'll do some sewing when she's not there.

Izzy thought about the mint green dress and wondered if it had belonged to Grace and if so, had she made it herself and where had she worn it? Izzy had a few beautiful dresses, pushed to the back of the wardrobe, all bought for work functions she'd had to attend with Jason. All those nights of making small talk with dull people, always with a smile on her face. Always there to provide support, something that rarely happened the other way around. Izzy hadn't worn any of them since. She was about to turn the page when she realised what she'd just read. Grace's married name would be Barclay, the same last name as Hettie.

29 June 1919

News travels fast. At the grocery store today, I had three people stop and congratulate me on my engagement to Martin. Yesterday, two of my cousins visited to say the same thing, and the day before that, our neighbours called in with good wishes. Mother said that after all the sadness in the past few years, an engagement gives people something to be happy about. I thought about what she said, and I think she's right. Everyone who has told me what wonderful news it is that I'm marrying Martin has someone in their family who didn't come home. It must be terrible to live with that. I had a cousin who died somewhere called Pozieres. I'd only met him twice because he lived on a property near Longreach. We travelled there once when I was a child, and it was such a long way. Mother didn't enjoy the journey, so we didn't do it again. He and his family came to visit us once. I can't remember why. It was many years ago now. So I didn't feel sad when Mother told me he'd died because I hardly knew him. Mother and Father are lucky that my brother Frank didn't go; otherwise, he might

not have returned. Or he might have gone and come back a different person as Martin has.

Izzy flicked through the pages of the diary, looking for any references to what Martin was like before he went off to war, but she couldn't find any. There was no mention of him at all for several weeks.

20 August 1919

Mother and Father held a small dinner for Martin and me to celebrate our engagement. Martin's parents were there, and so were my brother and his wife. Father made a speech, and Martin also said a few words. Father spoke more about welcoming Martin to our family and the excellent job he was doing at the factory than he did about me. Martin said how happy it had made him when I agreed to marry him and how he was looking forward to our life together. Susannah, my sister-in-law, reached across the table, held my hand and told me how content I'll be. Frank said something similar to Martin, although in a more matter of fact way. I made a new dress for the dinner. It's buttercup yellow with lace and some delicate beadwork. Susannah couldn't stop admiring it and said I had a talent for sewing. She also admired my ring. It's a gold band with small diamonds on the sides, leading up to a single, larger, round diamond at the top. Before dinner was over, Bryce, the factory foreman, came in. He needed to speak to Father. I overheard him say one of the workers had been caught stealing, and Bryce had fired him. Before he left, he apologised for interrupting, and he congratulated Martin and me on our engagement. I thought that was very nice of him. Bryce always has good manners.

Izzy put down the diary and then picked it up again to make sure she'd read the name right. Bryce.

Chapter Three

"Either you weren't telling the truth, or you're a natural," Trent said.

"Beginners luck, maybe."

They were on the sixth hole, and so far, she hadn't done anything to embarrass herself. In fact, she was pleased with how well she was playing, something the scorecard reflected. Trent had borrowed a set of ladies' golf clubs and given her a few pointers on when and how to use them. The longer they played, the more she wished she'd tried the game sooner. But golf had been Jason's game, and whenever Izzy mentioned taking it up, he'd been very dismissive of the idea. Eventually, she'd dropped the subject. Like so many other subjects she'd dropped over the years.

"That was a great shot," Trent said.

"For a minute, I thought the ball would end up in the water, not over it."

"If it did, it could keep mine company."

Izzy laughed and then got back in the cart to head further down the fairway.

"You should think about taking up golf. You have a talent for it."

"Thanks. And thanks for inviting me."

"I'm sure this won't be our only game."

Izzy turned and pretended she was looking at the course. Was he as interested as he seemed? Or was she being fooled again?

After the game, they headed into the clubhouse for a drink, which was interrupted by other players stopping to say hello to Trent. And to also ask who his playing companion was. Each time he introduced her, he smiled. Each time she took another sip of her drink, hoping that no one else would come over. It was getting too much for a second date, although if she counted the BBQ at Teresa's, it was the third occasion where they'd spent time together. As he walked her back to her car twenty minutes later, he asked her to dinner and a movie on Friday night.

"I already have plans on Friday."

"How about the following Friday?"

Izzy nodded. "Ok."

After dinner at Teresa's that night, and after Rob had taken the kids to the movie room they had downstairs, Izzy told her about the golf game.

"Sounds like another good date to me. And it's also a good sign that Trent was courteous and helpful, but not condescending, while you were playing. It says a lot about him."

Izzy nodded.

"So why did you tell him you had something on this Friday night when you don't?"

"I don't know. I panicked, I guess."

"Why?"

"It's going too fast. I'm not ready."

"Then just tell him that."

"I can't tell him that. We've only been on two actual dates."

"You don't have to go into detail."

"But what if he asks? I don't want to lie, but I don't want to tell him the truth either."

"What happened was awful, but you can't let that stop you."

"Why not?"

"You're not the one who did the wrong thing. So why should Jason get to move on while you're still stuck where you were two years ago."

Just the sound of his name made Izzy feel sick. "Can we change the subject?"

Teresa reached over and squeezed Izzy's hand. "Of course. Did you bring one of the diaries? I'd love to read some more."

Izzy reached into her bag and pulled out the diary she'd brought with her. As she turned the pages, she filled Teresa in on what she'd read so far. When she got to the page she was up to, Teresa topped up their wine glasses, the contents coming out of a bottle from their cellar, and they sat back and read the next entry.

11 September 1919

Plans are going ahead for the wedding. I haven't told anyone of my feelings. I'm not even sure of them myself. I know the wedding will go ahead and I will marry Martin and stay married for the rest of our lives. That's what people do. I am happy about it, and I'm sure we will be happy together. But there is a part of me that wishes there was another option. I will go from being the daughter of my parents to the wife of Martin. Will I ever get a chance to be a person in my own right?

At least she wasn't the only one who had mixed emotions, even if they were a hundred year's apart, Izzy thought to herself. She turned to look at Teresa.

"Her words are so sad."

Teresa nodded. "I certainly never felt that way. I was excited about getting married and spending the rest of my life with Rob. It's not always smooth sailing, but it's still one of the best decisions I've ever made."

Izzy sighed. "Not a decision I've had to make yet."

Teresa reached over and squeezed Izzy's hand again. "Sorry, shouldn't have said that."

Izzy shook her head. "Don't be silly. Nothing to be sorry about. Let's see what else Grace had to say."

     The Diary and the Green Dress

I have spent a lot of time thinking about the wedding. Martin is an honest, hardworking man, and he has always treated me well. Over the past few weeks, I have been talking with Susannah. She has been married to Frank for six years, and she said she's never been happier and couldn't imagine not being a wife and mother. After talking with her, I started to think that maybe I had the wrong idea about marriage and that after I am Martin's wife, I too will be happier than I have ever been. Mother always tells me how lucky I am to have a man like Martin about to become my husband. I know she's right. Some women have terrible husbands. I have seen them; the ones who look hungry all the time because their husbands have spent all their money on drink, the ones whose husbands are in and out of work. So they wear the same clothes each year, with more mending visible than the year before. The worst is the woman I saw one day in the front yard of her house. She had a bruise on her face, and when she saw me looking at her, she quickly turned around and went inside. It wasn't the first time I'd seen her like that either. I wanted to knock on the door and see if there was anything I could do, but I didn't. No one does. It's an unwritten rule that we all stay out of everyone else's business.

"That poor woman," Izzy said.

"Guess things haven't changed that much in one hundred years."

Izzy turned to look at her friend.

"What?" Teresa said. "Oh, no, I wasn't talking about me. I just meant we have both known women over the years that have been in the same terrible situation."

Izzy nodded as she picked up the diary again. Too many, she thought to herself. At least now there were options available, even if some of them weren't that good or available to all the women that needed them. The woman Grace had written about would have had no option at all. And given the era Grace was writing in, if the woman had asked for help, she probably would have been told that the man who did that to her was her husband. She had to stay with him, no matter what.

14 October 1919

> *Martin came to the house today to take me for a walk. It was lovely strolling under the trees that line the footpath. Quite a few people were doing the same thing as we left our street and turned onto the main road. Unfortunately, the first person we ran into was Mrs Robertson, who plays the organ at church. We'd barely said hello when she asked if we'd thought about what song we'd like her to play before the Wedding March while people were waiting for me to enter the church. We haven't spoken to her about the wedding, but she already presumes she will be part of our service. I don't even like organ music! Martin was polite but ended the conversation soon after, telling her he had to get me home by a particular time. I was glad that was the end of it. But then, a bit further along, we ran into Mrs Stephens. I know it's uncharitable, but I don't like her. She fusses so much about every little thing. But she's on the church fete committee with Mother, so we stopped and talked with her. She wanted to know about the wedding too. It seems to be the only topic of conversation anyone is interested in since Martin and I became engaged. I told her Mother and I had all the plans in hand. She kept pressing for details, and I didn't want to tell her because it would be all over town by the end of the day if I did.*

16 October 1919

> *I had dinner with Martin tonight. He came over, and Mother and Father let us have dinner in private. He didn't mention the wedding, and he seemed quieter than usual. I wonder if he's having second thoughts. I wish I'd had the courage to ask him. But, instead, I continued to eat my dinner.*

"I can't imagine not asking a question like that if you were about to get married," Izzy said.

"Maybe women didn't ask questions like that back then," Teresa said. "Or maybe she was afraid of the answer. After all, the fact they were getting married was widely known. It would have been a difficult decision to call it off."

"Better to be called off than go ahead if it's not the right thing to do."

Izzy looked down again at what Grace had written. When the

    <u>The Diary and the Green Dress</u>

subject had come up with Jason, she'd asked questions. It hadn't done her any good, but she'd still asked. Unfortunately for her, he'd been a terrific liar.

"What does the rest of the entry say?" Teresa said.

Maybe it was something else occupying his mind. I know he's been busy at work. Father told me that. He also met with someone he was in France with yesterday. I saw Martin afterwards, and he was very quiet. When I asked if he'd enjoyed catching up with the man, he looked at me for a moment before saying enjoyment wasn't the reason they sometimes see each other. I asked why they meet up then, and he said I wouldn't understand. I've asked a few times about what happened in France, but he keeps saying it's over now, and there's no need to talk about it.

Izzy put down the diary. "I've got to go to the bathroom. Have a look and see if you can find the next mention of Martin."

Once Izzy shut the door, she leaned against the wall. Surely there couldn't be many more entries about weddings. She should have left the diary at home and said she'd forgotten it. But she'd been friends with Teresa long enough to realise that she would want to know everything Grace had written. So she may as well get these entries over and done with, and they could move on to something else. Besides, it was better to read them with Teresa than on her own. She was less likely to cry that way, and if she did, at least Teresa would hand her a tissue.

"Got it," Teresa said as Izzy sat back down and tucked her feet up underneath her. "It wasn't hard to find. It's on the next page."

19 October 1919

Martin and I stayed back after church this morning. Father Stewart wanted to talk to us about the wedding. He said he was very happy for us, and it pleased him to see two nice people commit their lives to each other before God. Martin didn't say very much, which I thought was strange because he has known Father Stewart since he was a child, as have I. He christened both of us. I began to wonder again if Martin has changed his mind. Father Stewart asked him if everything was all right now that he had been home since the beginning of the year. Martin said things were fine and then turned and said we had to go. It seemed very rude to me, the way he acted. The look on Father Stewart's face told me he thought the same, even though the look passed quickly before anyone else could see it but me.

23 October 1919

I lay awake for a long time last night thinking about the way Martin behaved after church. That hasn't been the only time recently when he hasn't seemed himself. On Monday, he called in on his way home from work to talk to Father. They spent an hour in Father's study, and when he left, he barely acknowledged me. Yet, when I waved goodbye from the window, he stood outside for few moments, looking up at me smiling, before waving back and then turning and walking away. And the Thursday night, when Martin came for dinner, he spoke to me quietly before he left and said he couldn't imagine our life together causing any unhappiness for anyone. Mother and Father came back into the room just after he said it, and he hasn't said anything like that since.

Beside her, Teresa started yawning. "Sorry, I was up early this morning."

"That's all right. I've had a long day too, so I might head off."

"Thought you must have. You've been quieter than usual tonight."

"Just tired."

"I'm dying to know what happens next. Make sure you text me when you've read the next few entries."

Izzy smiled. "Will do."

On the way out, Izzy turned and hugged her friend, and for a moment, she wondered if she should tell Teresa her news. But how could she when she'd only just found out about Claudia herself?

Chapter Four

Two weeks later, she still hadn't said anything to Teresa. And as Trent arrived to pick her up for their third official date, she knew she wouldn't be saying anything to him either. So instead, she decided to tell him about the diaries. At least that would stop the other thoughts that had been racing through her mind. After dinner and the movie, they were still talking about them.

"What are the chances of something like that being left in your house? Especially if they were written by someone who lived there."

It had occurred to Izzy that might be the case, but there were many other reasons they could have ended up there. Just because there was a connection between Grace and Hettie didn't mean that Grace had ever lived in the house. She hoped Grace had, though. The thought that she was reading something written by someone who had lived in her home, even if it was only for a short time, was exciting.

"All that was left in my house when I moved in was an old broom in the shed and a cracked bucket in the laundry."

Izzy laughed. "I think my find is slightly more exciting."

Trent laughed too. "Yes. I just added mine to a load of rubbish I took to the dump. But who knows what you'll find as you keep reading? If they were written by a previous owner, there could be all sorts of interesting information about your house, maybe even a mystery or a few surprises."

Surprises were not what Izzy wanted to think about. But, in one sentence, Trent had managed to bring back all the thoughts she'd been trying to block all night. The same ones she'd been trying to ignore for the past two and a half weeks.

"You'll have to read more and then update me on Sunday night."

"What's on Sunday night?"

"Our fourth date if you don't already have plans. There's a show on at the Powerhouse that's been getting good reviews."

Izzy watched as he drove away, wondering whether she should have agreed to a fourth date so soon. But ever since he'd mentioned surprises, all she could think about was Claudia. And thinking about Claudia was far more complex than thinking about whether two dates in three nights was too much. Izzy sighed. Life had been the same for two years, and then in the space of two months, she'd bought a house, met Trent and found out about Claudia. What she needed was a break from her thoughts. She turned on the TV, but nothing appealed to her. She picked up the book she'd been reading, but that didn't hold her interest either. Eventually, she picked up the diary. Even though the entries on the following few pages were about the wedding, at least she'd be thinking about Grace's life for a while and not her own.

10 November 1919

Mother and I had a cup of tea in the drawing-room this afternoon. We don't do this very often as Mother is busy in the afternoons with her charitable work. I enjoyed spending time with her, but Martin and our upcoming marriage were the main topics of conversation. She told me again that she hoped I realised how lucky I was to be marrying Martin. The ladies on her charity committee said the same thing the last time they met here at the house. And like Mother, they also told me that twenty was a good age to get married.

15 November 1919

I visited Susannah today. She was very tired as her youngest was sick and had been up all night. I made her a cup of tea, and she sat down with me to drink it. She drank it so fast that I made her another one straight away. As she drank the second cup, she asked me about the final wedding preparations. I'll be glad when the wedding is over so there can be a different topic of conversation. I then did something I'd thought about the whole time I was walking to her house. I asked her if she was happy. I know she's said before that she is, but did she mean it? She looked at me for a few moments and then nodded and said most of the time. When I

    <u>The Diary and the Green Dress</u>

asked her about the other times, she said it didn't matter and that she was content to just look after her husband and children. As soon as she said it, she changed the subject.

20 November 1919

The wedding is only two days away, and everything is organised. Mother said all I have to do is put on my dress and go to the church. Father said he was proud to be walking me down the aisle. Everyone we invited is coming. I keep thinking I should be more excited. I haven't been able to think of anything but Susannah since I visited her.

22 November 1919

I am getting married today. My dress is hanging up, ready to wear. It took longer to make than I expected, but it's beautiful, and I can't wait to wear it. Mother came to speak to me last night. She tried to explain what would happen on my wedding night, what Martin would expect. She didn't explain very much but said it was my duty as a wife to do what he expects. I knew what she was referring to. Some of my married friends are quite modern and have spoken to me about what will happen and what I should do. It doesn't sound as bad as what Mother said it will be. I'll know after tonight. I do love Martin, and I will be happy being his wife. I'm sure I will.

Izzy got up off the bed and pulled the mint green dress out of the wardrobe. If Grace had made it, then she could only imagine that her wedding dress would have been exquisite. It was a pity there were no photos. Even though weddings weren't her favourite topic of conversation, she would have loved to see the dress Grace made for the day. She stared at the dress for a few more minutes but eventually, yawning got the better of her. Her body, and her mind, needed a rest.

The next afternoon Izzy pulled the green dress out of the wardrobe again. She'd been thinking about it during the day, wondering if there would ever be an occasion to wear it. It would need repairs first, but Izzy didn't think it would be hard to fix if she could find someone good at repairing vintage dresses. She ran her hand along the soft material, thinking that if Grace and Martin had lived here at some point, and it was Grace's dress, she would have walked through the rooms wearing it. If she had, what did the house look like back then? What sort of furniture had been here? What colour were the curtains? Teresa had mentioned that it might be worth visiting the local historical society to see what information they had on the area and if there was anything available about her house. That would be something else she could do to take her mind off Claudia, except that Claudia would be the main topic of conversation tonight. Izzy needed to talk to someone, so she'd rung Teresa and asked her to come over. She hadn't told her why.

"Ok, what's going on?" Teresa said. "You were quite adamant on the phone that you needed to talk to me tonight."

"I need to sit down first."

Teresa waited, but Izzy didn't say anything more.

Finally, after a few minutes, Teresa said, "Izzy, you are making me feel uneasy, so you had better start talking."

Izzy thought back to the night, almost three weeks ago now, when her parents had invited her over. She remembered every detail.

Izzy had hugged both her parents as she'd walked through the door. "What's the important news that couldn't wait until our lunch this weekend?"

Neither of them said anything. Instead, they just looked at each other and then at Izzy.

"What is it?"

Her parents looked at each other again, and then her dad spoke. "There's something we need to tell you."

"Ok."

For the third time, her parents looked at each other.

"I'm getting worried now. Is it health-related?"

They both shook their heads.

"Thank goodness for that. Is it something to do with money?"

They both shook their heads again.

     The Diary and the Green Dress

"I'm not asking any more questions. Just tell me."

Silence filled the room before her dad took a deep breath. "You have a half-sister."

Izzy looked from one to the other. "What?"

"You have a half-sister."

"I don't understand."

"When I was at university, I had a girlfriend. She was from Germany and went back there when she finished her degree. She didn't know at the time she was pregnant."

Izzy's mum turned away but not before Izzy could see the tears forming in her eyes.

"Didn't she try and contact you?"

Her dad nodded. "But my parents and I moved a few weeks after she left the country, so she didn't know how to contact me."

"How did she find you now?"

"She didn't. Claudia did."

Izzy sat back in the chair. Claudia.

"Why did she contact you now? And how did she find you?"

"Her youngest child has a medical condition, and she needed to research the family medical history. So she searched the Brisbane White Pages online and rang everyone with the same name as me."

"You've spoken to her?"

"Twice now."

"How long ago?"

"Last week. I've wanted to tell you since the first phone call, but I wasn't sure how to or how you would feel when you found out."

Izzy hadn't known how she felt, but that night after she'd arrived home, she'd spent the following hours trying to figure it out. And she hadn't slept at all.

Izzy looked up at Teresa. The whole time she'd been recounting the events of that night, she'd been looking at the floor.

"What! Of all the things I thought you might say, that wasn't one of them. How do you feel?"

"I'm still in shock."

"I'm sure your dad is too."

Izzy thought about the conversations she'd had with her dad since he'd told her. Shock was one of the emotions that had come up. So had anger at not finding out until now.

Izzy nodded. "And Mum isn't taking it well."

Teresa reached over and squeezed her hand. "You can only do what you can to support them. You can't forget your feelings."

Izzy knew Teresa was right, but it was hard to forget the tears in her mum's eyes. Just thinking about that made Izzy's eyes well up.

"Let's talk about something else for a while. There's plenty of time to talk more about Claudia when you're ready."

Izzy nodded.

"How are things going with Trent?"

Izzy laughed for the first time in a while. "I'm surprised you waited this long to ask."

"I just want to know if there's going to be a fourth date."

"Tomorrow night."

"Wonderful. Have you kissed yet?"

Izzy smiled. "Not telling."

     The Diary and the Green Dress

Teresa groaned. "Come on."

"Maybe I'll tell you some other time."

"Are you going to tell him about Claudia?"

Izzy shook her head. "Not yet."

Later that night, as Izzy lay in bed, all the feelings she'd had since finding out about Claudia came to the front of her mind. And the tears that had threatened to come earlier arrived in a flood.

Chapter Five

How are you feeling?

Izzy picked up her phone and put it down again three times before replying to Teresa's message. It was the fifth day she'd messaged asking the same question, but today, it took longer to find the right words to describe how she felt.

Unsettled. Dad had a video call with her this morning.

Can you talk?

About to go to a meeting.

I'll call you after work.

Izzy spent the next two hours only half-listening to the presentation about upcoming changes to the tax laws. She knew she should be paying attention as the changes applied to several of her clients. Nevertheless, her mind kept wandering back to the conversation with her dad. Claudia wanted to know about the time he'd spent with her mum, what she'd been like then, the things they'd done together, the places they used to go. He told her what he could remember as it was forty-two years ago. He also said that he knew Claudia's mum planned to go back to Germany after university. That the last time he'd seen her was when he waved goodbye at the airport. All of which she relayed to Teresa when she called later that day.

"I wonder how your dad felt seeing her for the last time as she headed towards her plane."

"I don't know. I didn't ask."

"I suppose it doesn't matter now. What does matter is that if they had a video call, he knows what Claudia looks like."

"Dad didn't say, and I couldn't ask, not when he'd only just seen her

     The Diary and the Green Dress

for the first time. I didn't want to make it harder for him."

"That's very considerate of you. I would have asked."

There'd been some consideration, but mostly, even though she'd initially toyed with the idea, Izzy wasn't ready to know if she and Claudia looked alike. And if Izzy found out what she looked like, that would be one more step in realising that she wasn't stuck in a dream and Claudia only a figment of her imagination.

"She didn't mention anything about contacting you?"

"Not that I know of."

As an only child, Izzy had always wanted a sibling, and all this time, she had one, or at least, a half-sibling. She'd had many friends growing up and some cousins that she would spend school holidays with, so she'd never been lonely. But to have someone that you saw every day, that you loved, fought with, grew up with, that was something different. She'd mentioned that to Teresa before, but she was one of five children, so she had a hard time understanding what it had been like for Izzy. They kept talking about the video call until Teresa picked up on the reticence in Izzy's voice.

"Have you read more of the diaries?"

"Not since the last time we spoke."

"Do you want to read me a couple of entries now?"

23 November 1919

The wedding went well. Mother helped with my dress and hair. The weather was lovely, and the sun shone through the stained-glass windows making the church very pretty inside. After the ceremony, we had delicious cakes and sandwiches. Everyone seemed happy for us, especially Martin's mother. She was smiling the whole day and told me she was glad that Martin had married someone as nice as me. We had some photographs taken and then it was over. The photographs were a novelty. It's only the third time in my life I've had my picture taken.

Izzy looked up from the diary and thought back to Teresa's wedding, where she'd been maid of honour. Teresa had been feeling nervous while they were getting ready, so they'd had a couple of glasses of champagne. By the time they got to the church, Teresa had forgotten about her nerves and almost skipped down the aisle. It had been a large wedding, full of fun and laughter. Jason had spent the day looking bored and kept asking her when they could leave. Finally, she persuaded him to stay until the end. Something he brought up every time Izzy wanted to leave somewhere before he did, despite it being the only time he'd stayed somewhere until the end because she wanted to. Usually, if he didn't want to stay, he'd leave, and she'd have to make her own way home.

"You still there?" Teresa said.

"Yes, sorry. I'll read the next bit."

Martin looked handsome in his suit. He is an attractive man and people told us we make a lovely looking couple. I was so pleased at how my dress turned out. It was perfect, exactly what I wanted. A lot of effort went into it, and it's such a shame that I'll never wear it again. Afterwards, Father helped Martin carry my belongings from where they sat neatly packed in the only house I've known, to what would be my house from now on. Martin helped me unpack some of my things and then said he was tired and wanted to go to bed. I felt nervous as I changed into my night-gown, but Martin went straight to sleep. I lay awake for a long time. I've never shared a bed with anyone, and it was strange. I listened to Martin breathing for a long time before I fell asleep. When I woke this morning, he wasn't in bed. After I got dressed, I found him in the kitchen, and I made him breakfast. We spent the day together setting up the house. The house belonged to my parents, but they gave it to us as a wedding gift, something Martin struggled with when they first said that's what they were going to do. I've always known that the factory was a successful business because we have had a privileged life, but I didn't realise it had done so well that my parents could give us a house. Martin's parents bought us some furni-ture, which was very kind of them and more than I expected. Even though they are very comfortable and have a lovely house, I suspect they spent more than they should have because of what my parents gave us. As well as the house, Mother and Father gave me a small desk and chair from their house. It's the one I've always used when I write in my diary. I put it in the small room at the back of the house. Martin said it was my room to

     The Diary and the Green Dress

use as I wanted. I put my sewing machine in there, and I can continue to write in my diary at the desk. It has a drawer I can keep it in.

"Damn," Teresa said. "I've got to go. Jack just spilled milk all over the kitchen floor."

After she hung up, Izzy looked down at the diary. She was starting to feel guilty reading the entries. But she figured Grace must have passed away a long time ago, so technically, she wasn't invading anyone's privacy. If Grace had known someone would read her diary one day, would she have written it the way she had? Or even written it at all? The only diary Izzy had was the one she wrote appointments in. This one was much more interesting.

24 November 1919

We were both tired after setting up the house yesterday and went to bed early. Martin went straight to sleep, and I lay awake for an hour or so. During the day, we also visited my parents. Martin is starting in his new position tomorrow after Father promoted him. It would have been nice to have a honeymoon, but Martin said we can do that later. He said he needed to prove himself at the factory and show Father that he'd made the right choice in giving him the promotion. He and Father spent a lot of time in the study talking about the business. I said I was interested too, but I wasn't included in the conversation. Father said I wouldn't understand what they were talking about. I would, though.

25 November 1919

Martin seemed pleased with how the day had gone. He said he enjoyed the new job and that the work itself was interesting. After dinner, we sat in the front room, and Martin read a book, and I did some sewing. We talked a little, and then Martin said he wanted to go to bed and asked me to go with him. I felt nervous, but I went. It hurt, but Martin was gentle. Afterwards, he said he'd wanted to wait a few days after the wedding so I could settle into the house. He also said it wouldn't hurt as much the next time. I hope he's right. I got out of bed as soon as Martin fell asleep. I needed to be by myself, so I've come to my room at the back of the house.

Izzy thought about the first time she'd had sex. Neither of them had any idea what they were doing, so it had been awkward, uncomfortable and over very quickly. If tomorrow night's date with Trent went well, she'd have to think seriously about asking him to stay the night. They were at that stage. But the next day at work, her mind was focused on a complicated tax return, and it wasn't until she was getting dressed for their date that she realised in a panic that she hadn't thought about it at all.

"I haven't been to this restaurant," Trent said as they walked in. "It was recommended to me. I hope it's good."

Izzy looked around at the exposed brick, gilt-edged mirrors and mahogany timber. "The restaurant looks beautiful. I'm sure the food will be too."

"It looks like a Parisian bistro."

"Have you been to Paris?"

Trent nodded. "A long time ago. It was on one of those bus tours where you cram as much of Europe into six weeks as you can. What about you?"

Izzy shook her head. "It's somewhere I've always wanted to go. Just haven't had the chance yet."

"I'd like to go back. Visiting the city as part of a bus tour that was more about drinking than sightseeing wasn't the best way to experience it. I'd like to go back to Germany too. Thinking back now, I mostly remember the beer."

Izzy followed the waiter to their table and sat down. She didn't say anything for a few minutes.

Trent reached over and held her hand. "Are you ok?"

For days afterwards, she wasn't sure if it was just the mention of Germany or if it was something else that made her reveal Claudia's existence.

"Wow. I can't imagine finding out something like that. Have you spoken to her?"

     <u>The Diary and the Green Dress</u>

Izzy shook her head.

"Do you think you will?"

"Maybe. I'll wait and see. The menu looks great."

As far as Izzy was concerned, that was enough about Claudia. It was only their fifth date.

They stayed at the table and talked for longer than either of them realised. It was only after the waiter came and asked if he could get them anything else that they looked around and saw they were the last ones in the restaurant.

Trent smiled. "I think the waiter would like us to leave."

Izzy smiled too. "I think you're right."

As they got in the car, Izzy looked over at Trent and decided at that moment she would ask him to stay.

The following morning, as she lay in bed and thought about what happened after they got back to her place, she was glad she'd made that decision. And when Trent offered to get up and make the coffee, she could only smile and nod. After he left the bedroom, she got up, got dressed and headed out to the verandah. As she waited, her phone beeped. She picked it up and looked at the message, and laughed. It was from Teresa, and all it said was 'so…*did you?*'

"Here you go," Trent said, handing Izzy her coffee.

"Thank you."

"There's a great view from here."

Izzy nodded, looking out at the same hills, houses and trees she'd seen when she'd first inspected the house. "I sit out here a lot."

"That railing looks a bit loose."

"Yes, it's on the list of things to fix. Old Queenslanders are beautiful, but there's always work to be done."

"I'll bring my toolbox next time and fix it for you. If you're happy to have a next time."

Izzy smiled. "That would be wonderful."

They sat on the verandah and chatted until it was time for Trent to leave so he could get to his golf game on time. Then, as she watched him drive away, she thought to herself, maybe this will be okay. It was a thought that stuck with her during the day as she caught up on the household chores she'd been putting off. At least thinking about Trent took her mind off how much she hated cleaning the bathroom.

By late afternoon she'd had enough of cleaning and washing and grocery shopping. So she made herself a coffee, grabbed the diary she was halfway through and headed out to the verandah. There were pages of entries about everyday things, so Izzy flicked through them until she found something she knew she'd have to share with Teresa.

     The Diary and the Green Dress

Chapter Six

3 February 1920

I've been unwell for the past few days. Mother said I just need to rest. She keeps looking at me as if she wants to say something but then doesn't. And she keeps telling Martin that he has to be tender with me. I've never heard her say anything like that before. Maybe she's just concerned because I've been so sick, and I'm not sure what it is. Whatever it is, I hope it stops soon. I'm tired of vomiting and not being able to keep my food down. Bryce drove Martin home from the factory last night, and he called out from the front door to say he hoped I'd feel better soon. It was nice of him to say that.

"It was going to happen at some point," Teresa said down the phone. "She must have had some idea."

"Not from the sounds of that entry."

"Keep reading. She'll figure it out soon enough."

"Have you got the time?"

"I'm supposed to be reading Jack and Rosie a story, but they're distracted at the moment. I don't know how long I've got, so you better start."

17 February 1920

I'm glad to be out of bed and doing things again. The past two weeks have been terrible, not being able to do anything but rest. Even reading a book made me feel tired. Martin asked me if I felt well enough last night to go to bed together. I said yes even though I didn't want to. It still hurts sometimes, but not as bad as that first time. I wonder how often I'm going to have to let Martin do that?

"Poor woman," Teresa said. "Didn't she know you're supposed to enjoy sex?"

"I guess she didn't. Maybe it gets better for her at some point."

"Hope so. Maybe Martin was no good."

"Or maybe he just thought about himself and didn't worry about Grace."

"Wouldn't be the first guy to do that."

"No."

"But that's not something you have to worry about."

"We're not talking about me at the moment. Back to the diary."

"Ok, but skip any entries that don't look interesting. I think I'm running out of time."

20 March 1920

After a few weeks of feeling better, I've been sick again. Martin seems worried about me, but Mother doesn't, which is unusual. She fussed over me when I first became sick, but now, she tells me that my sickness is normal. I'm not sure why it would be considered normal. I've tried asking her what she means by that, but she just says I'll know soon enough.

30 March 1920

I spoke to Mother again and said I wasn't going to stop asking until she told me why she thinks my sickness is normal. She hesitated but finally said she thinks I'm pregnant. When I asked her why she hadn't said that before, she said she wanted to wait in case there was another reason. She didn't want to get my hopes up if the pregnancy wasn't the cause of my sickness. Over the past few days, it occurred to me that I might be pregnant. I don't know if I'm ready to have a child. I wonder how Martin will react?

I haven't told Martin yet. Mother said to wait a bit longer. I wish I could do something about the sickness, although at least now it's only for a few hours in the morning rather than all day like it was. Mother made me a drink with ginger in it, which helps, but she said I just have to wait for it to pass.

That was the last entry. After Izzy finished talking to Teresa, she put that diary back in the drawer, took the next one from the top of the pile and put it beside her bed for another time. All she wanted now was to have a long bath, then put on her pyjamas, order takeaway and sit in front of the TV by herself. She'd done enough talking over the past few days.

"Morning, Harry," Izzy said as she waved to him over the fence the following day. "Back from your morning walk?"

Harry nodded. "Have to keep that up every day. It's important at my age. I go a bit further on Sundays, down to the newsagent on the main road to get myself a newspaper."

Izzy smiled. "I should get into the habit of a daily walk."

"Walking is excellent exercise. And the best part is the cup of tea I have when I finish."

"I'll make you one if you like."

"That would be nice. A cup of tea always goes better with a chat."

While Izzy made him a cup of tea, and a coffee for herself, Harry walked around her lounge and dining rooms.

"You've set these rooms up nicely."

"Thank you."

"I've always liked this house, but I've never been inside."

"You're welcome to have a look at the other rooms."

Harry shook his head. "If I do, I won't have an excuse to come back for another visit."

Izzy smiled. "You're welcome to come over anytime. Here's your tea. Shall we sit outside on the verandah?"

Harry nodded and followed her out. "How do you like the neighbourhood so far?"

"It's great. So quiet, which I didn't expect to find this close to the city."

"Yes, although it's not as quiet as it used to be. There are a lot more houses now, and the blocks are smaller. No one has a big backyard anymore."

"A lot of suburbs are like that now. I'm not sure I'd want anything bigger than what I've got. It's enough to look after by myself."

"Your yard used to be bigger, but your house was moved up the block, and then the block was divided and the other half sold. That house next door on the low side has only been there for twenty-five years."

Izzy peered over the railing into the yard next door and then turned around to look at her yard, trying to imagine what it would have looked like when it was all one large block. If the house was still further down in the middle of the block as it had been, then some of the tall, lush trees that were next door would be hers. The three planted close together near the fence line would be a perfect spot to put some outdoor furniture. Nestled against the thick trunks underneath the green canopy, providing shade all day long. Izzy could picture herself sitting there with a book, or now that she had the diaries, with one of those. It looked like such a peaceful spot. Izzy wondered if Hettie, or Grace if she had actually lived in the house, ever sat there on a hot summer's day. Escaping from the heat and humidity that is so common during a Queensland summer, especially as there would have been no air-conditioning. In Grace's case, she would have been wearing clothes that, while appropriate for the time, would not have been appropriate for the time of year. And as Izzy looked more closely at the gardens next door, she could see similarities in the layout between it and her own garden, which made sense as moving the house would have been after Grace's time, so it would have been Hettie who'd done it and she questioned why. She hoped it wasn't because she needed the money. It would be sad to think Hettie had to give up some of her lovely gardens. She

     The Diary and the Green Dress

asked Harry if he knew why, but he shook his head. He remembered Hettie as someone who didn't speak about things happening in her life, a private person who kept their conversations brief, friendly but brief, never going into details. As Izzy listened to him, she knew she'd have to keep asking him questions. There were so many things he knew. She didn't mention the letter, though. She wasn't sure what it meant that someone named Bryce wrote to Grace and mentioned Hettie. If Hettie had been as private as Harry said, then it's unlikely she'd ever mentioned the name Bryce to him. If she knew who he was, that is.

"Thanks for the tea," Harry said as he stood up. "It was very nice, but I have to be going. I've got a lot to get done today."

It was only after he'd gone that Izzy realised he might know if Grace had ever owned Izzy's house, and if she had, she still might have been living in it when Harry moved next door.

"I can't believe you didn't ask him."

Izzy sighed down the phone. She knew Teresa would say that.

"I didn't think about it until after he went."

"Considering how long he's lived in his house, he might have known her."

"We don't know how long Grace lived here if she did at all. We're not even sure what the relationship between Grace and Hettie was yet. Just because they had the same last name doesn't mean they were mother and daughter. Hettie could have been Grace's niece for all we know."

"Harry probably knows."

Izzy sighed again. "He's only next door. I can ask him at any time."

"The sooner, the better. Go over now."

"I'm not going over now. It's late, and he's probably asleep."

"I suppose you're right. Have you read anymore of the diaries?"

"Not since the last one I read to you."

"Well, you better hurry up with that too. The more we find out, the more I want to know."

Izzy laughed. "We find out?"

"Ok, so it's mostly you finding out then telling me. Now, are things still going well with Trent?"

Izzy had been waiting for that question. After all, it had been a few days since Teresa had asked, which was remarkably restrained for her. Izzy knew she kept asking because she wanted her to be happy. Still, their main topics of conversation lately were either Trent or the diaries. It wouldn't be long before Claudia joined the list on a more frequent basis, but for now, she'd made it clear she wasn't ready for that. Teresa had always been one to share every detail of her life, so she found it hard to understand why Izzy didn't want to talk about Claudia more. But Izzy wasn't like that; she constantly juggled what to say and what not to say.

The following afternoon, after spending most of the day cursing under her breath that she hadn't asked Harry if he'd known Grace, she left work early and went over to his house with a packet of biscuits.

"I went for a long walk this morning before work," Izzy said as she sat down, taking the cup of coffee Harry was handing to her.

Harry smiled. "Good."

"There are some very nice homes in the neighbourhood, including yours. It's beautiful."

"Thank you. I built it myself."

"Really? That's amazing. You must have put a lot of time and effort into it."

"I did, but it was worth it. We were happy here for so many years, and I won't be leaving until my time is up. This is my home."

Izzy waited until Harry had finished the biscuit he was eating before asking the question she'd been thinking about since he'd left her verandah the day before.

     The Diary and the Green Dress

"Did you ever meet someone at my house named Grace?"

"Yes, a lady name Grace owned your house when I was building and for many years after that. The house went to her daughter Hettie after she passed away."

Izzy could barely contain her excitement. She was talking to someone who'd met Grace. And he'd solved the relationship puzzle between Grace and Hettie in just a few words. Again, she started cursing that she hadn't asked him sooner. She told him she'd found some of Grace's diaries and that she'd started reading them.

"I wouldn't say I knew Grace well. We talked over the fence as neighbours do, but that was about it. She was a private person but spoke to me more than Hettie ever did. I never met Martin. He died before I bought this block of land."

Later, after she got home, she began to wonder how and when Martin had died. It must have been a long time before Grace if Harry had known her but not him. She wasn't seeing Trent that night, and after she'd cooked herself dinner, she tossed up whether to watch TV or read more diary entries. The diary entries won.

10 May 1920

I told Martin today. I was hoping he would be more excited. I don't think he's been excited about anything since he came back from the war. I thought maybe this would be what changed that, but even though he said he was happy at the news, something wasn't right. I tried to talk to him, but he went out for a walk instead.

18 May 1920

The news is out. Susannah was very excited and couldn't stop hugging me when I told her. Frank shook Martin's hand and said congratulations, then they started talking about a charity cricket match that is planned for later in the year. They're both playing in the game, and I think Martin was much happier to talk about that rather than the news we just shared. He didn't say much when we told his parents either. His parents, as with mine, seem more excited than Martin is.

The following few entries contained details of day-to-day things, like grocery shopping, washing and cleaning, so Izzy skipped a few pages.

12 June 1920

We went for a walk today. It took a lot of convincing before we went. Martin kept saying I'm supposed to be resting, but I've done very little except rest, and I wanted to go for a stroll. We'd only gone a short way when we saw Mrs Stephens. She had us trapped for ten minutes, telling us all the ways I would need to care for the baby. I wanted to continue walking, but Martin seemed content to stay. I'm not sure, but I think he might have actually been listening to what Mrs Stephens was saying. Then she started talking about how important it was that I am careful. She had a tear in her eye as she told us her third baby had been born dead. I started to worry after she told us and then wondered why she would say something like that to me. When I mentioned it to Martin he didn't seem to think there was anything wrong with what she said. I've been thinking about it ever since.

13 June 1920

I mentioned the conversation with Mrs Stephens to Mother. She'd come to see me, and we were having a cup of tea in the kitchen. It's not a nice thing to hear, she said, but it happens. I looked at her and asked if it had happened to her. It took her a little while to answer. Then she just nodded and said it wasn't something she talked about. After a lot of persuading, she did, though. I found out I had another brother. He would have been eighteen months older than me. But when he was born, he wasn't breathing. I thought about what Mother had said after she left. What if that happens to me?

     The Diary and the Green Dress

Chapter Seven

Dear Isabel

If you're reading this, I assume you want to; otherwise, you would have deleted it as soon as you saw who it was from. I was unsure about sending you an email as I don't know how you feel now that you know I exist. However, from the conversations I've had with our father, I don't think he would have given me your email address if he thought I shouldn't contact you.

Izzy stopped reading the email. Our father. She said it repeatedly until it sunk in. Two words she'd never thought she'd hear. All her life, he'd just been her dad. Now there was someone else who could say the same thing. And she didn't like the sound of it.

I've known for a long time that the man who raised me was not my biological father. I didn't understand what that meant when I was young, but as I grew older and started asking questions, my mother always answered them honestly. As much as I love my stepfather, I always knew that I would try and find my biological father one day. Until now, I never felt ready to do so, then a reason came along, and I took it as a sign. I'd like to meet our father one day. And you, if you want to.

I know this is new for you, and you may need some time to process everything, but I hope you will reply to my email. I would like to hear from you and get to know you.

Claudia

Izzy put down her coffee cup. This was not how she expected to start her day. She read the email four more times before shutting down her computer and leaving for work. As she sat on the train, she went over every word in her head, hoping it would give her an idea of what she could say in reply. But it didn't help. She had no idea what to say. It didn't go unnoticed by her colleagues that something was on her mind. That day, of all days, the manager treated the firm's staff to lunch as a way of thanking them for all the hard work they'd been putting in. Usually, she would be the one keeping the conversation going, but the only thing she could think about was Claudia's email, and she certainly wouldn't be talking about that. More than once, the comment was made that she was very quiet, but each time it was said, she just replied by saying she hadn't slept well the night before. Which was partly true. She hadn't slept well since first finding out about Claudia.

It didn't go unnoticed by Trent either. All through dinner that night, she was quiet and when he asked her why she told him about the email.

"There's no rush to reply. It's taken this many years to find out. Take a few more days to decide how to respond. It won't make a difference."

He was right. Waiting a few days would also give Izzy time to think about what she wanted to ask. She wanted to know so much, but she couldn't ask everything in the first email, so she'd have to prioritise the questions running through her head. The question of meeting wouldn't be one of them, though. Not yet.

Trent started talking about his work trip to Melbourne, but Izzy was only half-listening, and she hoped he couldn't tell. As much as she tried to concentrate on what he said, the email kept creeping back into her thoughts. And also, as much as Izzy tried to be interested in IT, she couldn't do it. As long as her computer worked when she needed it to, she didn't care what was happening in the background. Not that she'd tell Trent that. He was very passionate about what he did. It was the same with her car—as long as it got her where she needed to go, she didn't care what was happening under the bonnet. She didn't say that to her mechanic either. When Trent finished, she told him about Harry. At least if she was talking about that, she wouldn't be thinking of something else. Or someone else.

"Did you tell him you found the diaries?" Trent asked when she'd finished.

Izzy nodded. "Like everyone else, he's interested too."

"Makes sense. History books only give you factual details, but

     <u>The Diary and the Green Dress</u>

something like this lets you discover what someone's life was like. Where are you up to?"

After the dishes were cleared away, Izzy got the diary and handed it to Trent.

22 June 1920

Susannah and the children came to visit today. The children were intrigued by the size of my stomach. Susannah deflected all the questions about how the baby got there. They kept asking though, and eventually, she sent them outside to the back verandah. I was glad she did. As much as I love them, they were noisy and wouldn't sit still, and it made me feel tired. From the look on Susannah's face, it was making her feel tired too. I asked her again if she was content just being a wife and mother. She didn't hesitate as much this time before she answered and said most of the time, the same as she said the first time I asked her. We talked about other things for a while, and then I asked her the same question I asked Mother. She shook her head in reply. I told her about the conversation with Mrs Stephens, and she was indignant, telling me Mrs Stephens had no business scaring me like that. Then she told me I'd be fine and there was no need to worry and that I would have a perfectly healthy baby. I nodded and reached over and squeezed her hand. I didn't say anything about Mother's reply to my question.

3 July 1920

Martin has been spending a lot of time at the factory lately. Some nights he doesn't come home until after I'm asleep. When I ask him about it, he says there is a lot to do. I don't remember Father ever working as late as Martin does. Bryce came by this afternoon to drop off some papers for Martin. I made him a cup of tea, and we talked while we waited for Martin to come back from a meeting with a supplier who is leaving by ship tomorrow for London. Even though I've known Bryce for several years, I've never had a long conversation with him before today. He's a lovely man and very intelligent. It was nice to talk with him. It was the longest and most interesting conversation I've had in a long time.

Trent got up to fill their wine glasses. "Seems a bit odd that Martin hasn't been spending time with his wife. Didn't they recently get married?"

Izzy nodded.

"If I was recently married and had a pregnant wife, I'd want to spend as much time with her as I could."

Izzy watched as he walked into the kitchen, trying not to let the doubts creep in. It was hard, though. How could she be sure she wasn't being fooled again? No matter how many times she said to herself she wasn't, the question kept coming back. So, as she'd done on several previous occasions, she dismissed the thought as quickly as she could and waited until he came back to start reading again. She had to stop letting past experiences cloud what could be her future.

14 July 1920

Bryce came by again today to discuss something with Martin. When I told him that Martin wasn't home yet, he commented on Martin's dedication to the factory. I just nodded in reply. I can't help think it's more than that. As with the last visit, we had a cup of tea and talked. I asked about his family. I met them once when they came to town. I can't remember why they came. I remember that his parents, especially his father, didn't like leaving the farm and coming to the city. I also remember that they were friendly people. He told me they were both doing well and that the farm was having a good year. He mentioned that his brother was getting married soon and that he'd spoken of going to Paris to live. Paris has always sounded romantic to me, but I don't think I'll ever get there. Martin has said he'll never go back to France, and from the way he said it, I don't think he'll ever change his mind.

"There's a lot of people to remember now," Trent said. "We've got Grace, Martin, their parents, and now Bryce and his parents and a brother. I wonder who else is going to appear in these diaries."

"Don't forget Grace's brother Frank as well as his wife, Susannah."

"I'll have to draw a family tree to keep it all straight. Do you think you'll reply to Claudia's email soon?"

Izzy turned to look at him but didn't say anything.

"Sorry. Back to the diary."

        <u>The Diary and the Green Dress</u>

We visited Martin's parents today. It's been more challenging for me to move as easily as I used to, so Father said Bryce could drive us in the factory car as it's easier to get into than the one Martin has bought. I still get excited when I go somewhere in a car. It's even more exciting to think that one day I might drive. Father and Martin are both of the view that women shouldn't drive, but I hope that one day they change their minds. Or that I find the courage to learn anyway. Frank and Susannah have a car, and I know Susannah has shown interest in learning to drive and that Frank isn't as opposed to the idea as Father and Martin. I know that when Susannah mentions it, she always says something about the children - what if something happened to one of them when Frank wasn't there to get them to the doctor. That might work with Martin, too, as he knows if you send for Dr Jackson, it takes a very long time for him to come. It's much quicker to go to him.

We stayed for lunch, and it was nice to spend time with Mr and Mrs Barclay. The food is always delicious at their house. They share a cook with their neighbour, and she is very good. Mrs Arthurs lost her husband in the war, and she supplements the money he left behind by cooking for others. She splits her days between the two houses—three days at each and then Sundays, she stays at home. After lunch, we all went outside for a cup of tea. Neither of Martin's parents drinks alcohol, not even an occasional port or sherry, but there is always a pot of tea on the stove. Mrs Barclay was full of questions about how I was feeling. Mr Barclay was interested too, saying he was looking forward to meeting his first grandchild. Martin hardly spoke the whole time we were there.

25 July 1920

I was thinking about yesterday. After Bryce dropped Martin back at the factory, he drove me home. He also asked how I was feeling. I told him I was feeling good and that it was very thoughtful of him to ask. He told me he had seven female cousins, so he'd spent a lot of time with women who were expecting a child. That made me think they must be a very close extended family, so I asked him, and we spent the rest of the drive home talking about Bryce's family. They see each other all the time, visiting each other's houses, going on picnics and more importantly, helping each other when they need it. Even though Bryce works in the city, he still goes home whenever he can. I asked him if he would go home and take over the farm one day. He shook his head. Much to my father's disappointment, he said, the farm life isn't for me. I asked him what would happen to the farm, and he said that one of his cousins would take it over. Will Martin take over the factory?

As Izzy turned the page, she heard a soft snore and looked beside her to see that Trent's eyes were closed and his head was lolling to one side. He'll be fine, she said to herself, just a few more entries. Then I'll put him to bed.

5 August 1920

Martin has been very busy at the factory, so Father asked Bryce to help with some things at the house now that I am unable due to my present condition. I know I shouldn't say it, but I look forward to his visits. He's delightful to be around and pays me more attention than Martin does. Yesterday he came to move some furniture out of the room that will soon be the nursery. There wasn't a lot of furniture in there and none of it heavy, so I could have done it myself, but everyone treats me like I'm very fragile when in fact, I've never felt stronger. I stood in the doorway after Bryce had removed the furniture and looked into the empty room, thinking that there would soon be a baby in there. It scares me to think that I will be responsible for another life. I tried to talk about that with Mother, but she brushed aside my concerns and said everything would come naturally to me. I must have had a strange look on my face because Bryce asked me if I was all right, and I told him what I'd been thinking. I haven't even mentioned it to Martin, but I told Bryce, and I didn't hesitate. It just came out. I felt so much better after talking to him. It was nice that someone didn't dismiss how I've been feeling.

4 September 1920

I'm very big now, and it's hard to move around. At least I don't have to wear a corset. That has been a blessing these past few months. Although I have heard that in Europe and America, they are falling out of fashion. I hope that happens here too and I never have to wear one again. They are torturous, and I still remember the first day Mother said I had

     <u>The Diary and the Green Dress</u>

to wear one. Even if they are falling out of fashion, I imagine Mother will continue to wear a corset for the rest of her life. She is very particular about things like that.

I haven't been able to stop thinking about my other brother. I wonder what he would have been like had he lived and how well we would have got along. I asked Mother how she felt when he was born not breathing, but she wouldn't tell me.

10 September 1920

I'm more tired than I ever thought I'd be. I'm not doing a lot, but everything I am doing is challenging. Martin is still spending a lot of time at the factory and still hasn't shown much interest in the fact that we'll soon have a child. I've asked a few times if he could help me get the nursery ready. The room has been empty since Bryce cleaned out the furniture. He always replies by saying he'll do it in the next few days, but nothing has happened.

18 September 1920

The nursery is finally done, although it wasn't Martin who moved the furniture into the room. I stopped asking him a few days ago and began thinking of how to get the furniture in there myself. I was trying to move some drawers when Bryce saw me through the open front door. He put down the papers he'd brought for Martin and came running down the hall. After getting me a glass of water and assisting me into a chair, Bryce moved everything into the room. I thanked him, and he said he was happy to help.

26 October 1920

Lily is beautiful. I didn't know I could love so much. Martin loves her very much, too, although he's nervous around her. I'm sure that will go in time. It's been three weeks now, and I feel relief that Martin changed so completely the first time he held her. I don't know what I would have done if he kept being distant. Mother has been here every day since Lily was born. She is sleeping now, and Mother is making me a cup of tea. This is the first chance I've had to write in my diary. I think the entries will be quite short for a while.

"So, did Trent stay again last night?"

Izzy could picture Teresa talking to her with a smile plastered across her face.

"Yes, he stayed."

"Things are continuing to go well then. Maybe I should give up my day job and become a matchmaker."

Izzy laughed. "It's probably a bit too soon to do that."

Teresa laughed too. "Maybe. Maybe not. I think I'm rather good at it. Have you responded to Claudia yet?"

"Not yet."

"Why not?"

"Because I'm not ready."

"Ok. But you'll let me know when you are?"

"Of course I will."

"And if you need some assistance in writing a reply, I'm happy to come over and help."

"Thanks. Now, I've got to hang up, or I'll be late for work."

Izzy knew Teresa was being helpful, but between her and Trent, she'd had enough questions about replying to Claudia. What do you say to a long-lost half-sister you never knew you had?

Two nights later, she stared at the computer screen for a long time, still trying to come up with the answer to that question. All she'd typed so far was *Dear Claudia.* That was as far as she'd got in twenty minutes. Although that wasn't strictly true. She'd written words but then deleted them. More than once. She wasn't moving, though, until she had words on the screen, even if it was a draft email she could read again and change later if need be, before sending.

I've read your email a few times now, as each time I read it, it

     <u>The Diary and the Green Dress</u>

becomes more real. I have a half-sister on the other side of the world. It's taken me a few days to respond because I haven't been sure what to say. I'm still not sure, but I could wait another week and not have the right words. I don't know how your mum told you about Dad, but I found out over a cup of coffee. Visiting my parents and chatting over coffee is something I do a lot, and it never occurred to me that this day would be any different. When I found out about you, my first reaction was shock. All these years, you were there, and I didn't know. The shock was followed by curiosity, and I wonder how similar we are. Did you feel the same or something different?

I hope you email back as I would like to get to know you too. And yes, it would be nice to meet one day.

Isabel

When she finished typing, she called Teresa, unsure about what she had written. And she wanted to make sure her split-second decision about wanting to meet was the right thing to add. She toyed with the idea of ringing Trent, but Teresa had known her longer and would give her the honesty she was looking for.

"Hit send," she said.

"Are you sure?"

"Yes, it's a good response. This is exciting."

"Exciting for you maybe, but scary for me. What if I don't hear back?"

"She's the one who initiated contact, so I'm sure she'll respond. Maybe she can come to Brisbane, and I could meet her too."

"Slow down. I haven't sent the email yet. Claudia might change her mind about meeting."

"I'm sure she won't. Promise you'll tell me when she responds?"

"You'll be the first to know."

After she hung up, Izzy stared at the screen for a few more minutes, looking at the mouse pointer hovering over the send button. Then her phone buzzed.

I was so distracted by you emailing Claudia that I forgot to ask about the diary.

Izzy looked down at the message on her phone and texted back a brief update.

What! She had the baby! I need to come over and read those entries and the ones after. How about tomorrow night?

Ok with me.

See you then. Have you sent the email?

Izzy read it one more time and then hit send.

Just then.

Woohoo! See you tomorrow night.

"Have you heard back from Claudia?" Teresa asked as she walked in the front door, still wearing the suit she'd worn to the office that day.

"I only sent the email yesterday."

"I can't believe how much you have going on at the moment."

Izzy sighed. "Sometimes, I wonder if it's too much."

"At least it's all good things. Now, where's the diary with the information about Lily?"

As Izzy handed the diary to Teresa, she couldn't stop thinking that it was too early to know whether Claudia coming into their lives was a good thing or a bad thing.

"I'm so glad Grace wrote about this," Teresa said when she'd finished. "How long have I got before Trent comes to pick you up for dinner?"

"He won't be here for another hour."

"Next diary then."

 <u>The Diary and the Green Dress</u>

1 December 1920

I'm glad I have a few minutes to write in my diary. Everything has been so hectic since Lily was born that I haven't written anything for weeks. Today, we ventured out of the house as a family for the first time. As much as I love Lily, it was nice to go outside and walk along the street instead of just walking around the house trying to settle her. We went to the Barclay's for lunch. Martin wanted to drive, but I wanted to walk. It took some convincing before he agreed, but it only takes twenty minutes, and it was such a beautiful day. We hadn't gone far when we saw Mrs Stephens. Of all people, it had to be her. Why do I always see her when I don't want to? She tried giving me advice, and I listened politely for as long as possible before telling her we had to go or we'd be late. She didn't listen and asked when the christening would be and if she could hold Lily. I said again that we had to go and started pushing the pram away.

7 December 1920

I didn't have time the other day to finish writing about visiting Mr and Mrs Barclay, so I will now. After we finally got away from Mrs Stephens, we ran into Mrs Robertson, the other person I didn't want to see. Are they the only two women who are going for a walk at the same time as Martin, Lily and I? As with Mrs Stephens, she was also full of advice. Since Lily was born, all I get from people is advice. There are no other topics of conversation. Luckily, she let us continue when I said we would be late. I spent the rest of the walk looking around me—at the trees, the parks, the buildings. I listened to the birds and the squeals of two children as they raced their bicycles down the road. I can't wait to see what Lily is like at that age.

16 December 1920

Tonight, we had dinner at Mother and Father's house. When we arrived, Bryce was there. He'd been talking to Father about factory business, and it had taken longer than expected, so Mother asked him to stay for dinner. He seemed pleased that he would be joining us. Dinner was lovely as it always is, and Lily slept peacefully throughout. Mother was hoping she'd wake as she wanted to hold her. Thankfully, it wasn't until I'd eaten the last mouthful of dessert that she did. Father wanted to hold her too, and I caught him smiling when he didn't think I was looking. Even Bryce wanted to hold her. He looked much more relaxed than Martin ever does. Those first few days after she was born, when I thought he'd changed, are now just a memory. He has gone back to being distant with me and hesitant around Lily. I know he loves her, but he can't seem to find a way to show it.

"Another mention of Bryce," Teresa said. "I hope there's more."

"What if there's not? If something was going on with him while she was married to Martin, she might not have written about it."

"I've just got a feeling there'll be something."

Izzy laughed. "I'm sure you do."

"Trust me. You'll read something in one of the diaries. Now, I better get going before Trent gets here. Don't want to get in the way."

"Why would you be in the way?"

"He's not going to kiss you properly if I'm standing here."

As she watched Teresa leave, Izzy hoped she never mentioned anything about her relationship with Trent at work. The more she thought about it, the more she knew Teresa would never do that. She took her job seriously and would never say or do anything inappropriate. It still felt odd that Teresa saw him every day, even if they just passed in a hallway, while Izzy was only seeing him a few times a week.

While waiting for Trent to arrive, Izzy went to her computer and held her finger above the power button. If there was a reply from Claudia, was she ready to read it?

Chapter Eight

Hello Isabel

I'm glad you replied. I've checked my emails more than usual since I wrote to you.

In answer to your questions, I wasn't shocked to find out I had a half-sister. I always assumed our father had a family.

Izzy shut down the computer. She didn't want to see those two words again so soon.

Later that night, after Trent was asleep and after she'd tossed and turned for several hours, she got up, went into the office and turned on the computer.

I was worried about what would happen when I contacted him, although I shouldn't have thought that way. Mother only ever says good things about him, and I've enjoyed our conversations. He always seems happy to hear from me. However, there is a small amount of doubt in my mind, so I hope you don't mind me asking, but as you know him so well, do you think he would have told me if he wanted nothing to do with me?

Claudia

P.S. yes, I do wonder how similar we are. Hopefully, one day we will get to find out.

The next morning, Trent made coffee, and they sat out on the verandah. There was a light breeze that cooled down the temperature. It was only 8 am, and already it was twenty-seven degrees. Ever since she'd moved in, she'd been debating about getting air conditioners installed. But the position of her house, high on a hill, meant that breezes were an almost everyday occurrence. There had only been a few days so far when the air had been so still that there had been no relief from the heat. It would be a considerable expense for a few days a year. And she wasn't keen on cutting any holes in her pressed metal ceilings or VJ walls.

"You seem quiet."

She hadn't told Trent about Claudia's email yet. She wanted to enjoy her coffee first. And get her thoughts straight in her head.

"Just tired. I didn't sleep very well."

"Morning, you two."

Izzy looked over the railing and saw Teresa at the front gate in her usual weekend attire.

"I didn't know you were coming over today."

"I wasn't planning to, but I finished the diary you lent me, so I thought I'd drop it back. Rob's taken the kids fishing, and you know how I feel about that."

Izzy remembered the one and only time Teresa had gone fishing with Rob. She'd hated picking up the worms to put on the hook, and she'd hated standing there for hours without catching a thing. Rob had asked once if Izzy would like to try fishing, but she politely declined after hearing about Teresa's experience.

"Did you find anything interesting in any of the entries?"

Teresa nodded, sat down on a chair and handed the diary to Izzy. "I've marked a couple of pages."

26 December 1920

Martin has taken Lily for a walk to try and get her to sleep. It's the only thing that works sometimes, and it's given me a chance to write about our lovely Christmas Day. Martin and I exchanged gifts next to the tree, and he'd wrapped a present for Lily. It was a pale pink bonnet that he'd asked his mother to knit. It will fit her perfectly when winter comes around. We went to Mother and Father's for Christmas lunch. They invited Mr and Mrs Barclay, and Frank and Susannah were there with their children. It was the strangest thing, but there was one empty chair at the table, and I kept looking at it, thinking how nice it would be if Bryce was sitting there.

    <u>The Diary and the Green Dress</u>

Unfortunately, he has gone to his parents' farm and won't be back for a few days. Bryce wished me Merry Christmas before he left and gave me a small present - a Christmas cake that one of his cousins made. He thought we'd enjoy it, and he didn't want it to go to waste while he was away. Christmas cakes last a long time, but maybe he doesn't know that. Frank and Susannah's children smiled and clapped their hands with joy as they opened their presents. Lily will be the same in a few years.

Izzy flicked through the pages until she came to the next one Teresa had marked.

16 January 1921

Lily's christening is today, and her gown is laying out ready. It's stunning. I'm glad it is because it took Mother and me a long time to make as the lace is very delicate. The church service is at 10 am, and then Mother and Father are hosting a lunch. We've chosen Frank and Susannah as godparents. Martin doesn't care who the godparents are and offered no suggestions. I don't think he wants a christening. He said something the other day about finding it hard to believe in God anymore. But he's going along with the christening because it's expected. At least he's wearing his best suit. We had a photo outside the church, the three of us. I don't have many photos, so this will be nice to add to the one taken at our wedding.

"I wish we knew what they looked like," Teresa said.

Izzy put the diary down. "Maybe we do."

She headed down the hallway to the spare room and then back again, shaking her head as she went. How could she have forgotten?

Trent looked down at the photos in her hand. "They're stuck to-gether."

Izzy nodded. "That's why I left them in the envelope in the trunk. I didn't want to damage them by trying to pull them apart."

"What if we tried holding them over steam?" Teresa said.

All three watched as Izzy held the photos above the kettle. Slowly, the corners started to come apart, and the first two photos were separated.

"It's a house," Izzy said. "But not this one."

A Victorian-era Queenslander, it was twice the size of Izzy's house. The grand front stairs climbed between two gas lampposts to a wide verandah encased with wrought iron railings, which surrounded the house. Three chimneys poked through an iron roof that rose in two levels, one covering the verandah and one covering the inside of the house. There were hedges along the front of the large yard, and to the left, they could see a smaller building made with the same timber as the house.

"Looks like a carriage house," Trent said.

Izzy turned the photo over. "*Mother and Father's house, Bowen Hills. 1892.*"

"I hope the house is still there," Teresa said. "It would be a shame to knock down something so beautiful."

"What's the next photo?" Trent said.

Izzy held it up to the light. "It looks like a picnic."

There was nothing written on the back, and the people in it had been too far away from the camera to distinguish any features. All they could tell was that it was an older man and woman and two younger couples. The six of them were sitting, the younger couples on a blanket and the older couple on chairs. To the right, three children were playing. The adults were looking at the camera, but the children were more interested in what they were doing to stop and pose. It was a shame that whoever had taken the photo had stood so far away. It was likely that it was Grace's family, but they couldn't be sure without anything written on the back.

Izzy held the last two photos over the steam, and after a few minutes, they came unstuck. She read what was written on the back of the first one and then turned it over.

"So that's what they looked like," Trent said.

It was the wedding photo Grace had written about. Even though Grace was sitting down, they could tell she was petite. She wore a floor-length white satin dress with capped lace sleeves and beading around the waist, along with a matching lace veil. The veil covered most of her hair and fell beside her ears, framing her oval face. They couldn't tell what colour her hair or eyes were as the photo was black and white. But the irises weren't dark, so they could only guess that her eye colour was something other than brown, and her hair looked fair so either light brown or blonde.

In contrast, Martin stood behind her, tall and stiff, like he was standing to attention. He was wearing a dark, pinstriped suit and vest, the colour of which was close to that of his hair. So both were either brown or black. Izzy looked closely at both their faces, but neither gave any hint as to what they thought as the photo was taken. Neither of them was smiling, but Izzy didn't think that was unusual given other photos she'd seen from that era. She tried to imagine what it would have been like having your photo taken back then. Compared to living in today's world, where everything and everyone is constantly photographed, she couldn't conceive how it would have felt. They were probably lucky they had this photo and the others they'd found. There would have been people back then who never had their photo taken; what they looked like lost to time.

"Grace, Martin and Lily?" Trent said as they looked at the last photo.

Izzy nodded. "Must be Lily's christening."

The white christening gown was long, completely covering Lily's legs, feet, and arms. There was a lace bonnet on her head, so it was hard to make out any of her features, let alone tell which one of her parents she most took after. The gown itself had lace around the neck, the ends of the sleeves and the hem. It looked very delicate and would have taken hours to make.

Teresa looked closely at the details of the gown. "Grace must have made the green dress."

"What green dress?" Trent asked.

Izzy took him down the hall to the bedroom and pulled the dress out of the wardrobe.

"I'd like to get it repaired one day and wear it."

"You'd need a special occasion."

Izzy nodded as she put the dress back in the wardrobe.

"I'm sure we can come up with something," Trent said.

She hoped he was right because the more she looked at it, the more she really wanted to wear it. But she couldn't think of an occasion coming up any time soon where she'd be able to wear something so exquisite and not be overdressed.

Teresa had made herself a coffee while they'd been looking at the dress and was out on the verandah drinking it when they came back. "You don't mind if I stay and finish this, do you? I don't get a chance to sit down and drink a whole cup of coffee very often."

"Of course not. Trent has to head off so you can keep me company."

As soon as Izzy shut the front door, Teresa put down her coffee cup.

"Nice to see Trent stayed the night again."

Izzy smiled. "Yes."

Something in the way she said it made Teresa suspicious. "What aren't you telling me?"

Izzy paused for a moment before speaking. "Trent told me he loved me last night. And it's not the first time he's said it."

"What! When was the first time?"

"The night you were here."

The one where I left because I said I didn't want to be in the way?"

Izzy nodded.

"Did you say it back?"

"Not the first time."

"But the second time?"

Izzy nodded again.

"This is big."

     The Diary and the Green Dress

"I know. And terrifying at the same time."

"He's not Jason."

"I know."

But she'd still thought about it carefully before she said the words back to Trent.

So, have you heard from Claudia?"

"Your two favourite topics of conversation at the moment are Trent and me and Claudia and me."

"Don't forget the diaries. As for you and Trent, I like seeing you happy. Besides, I've been married so long now I've forgotten what it's like to go on a date."

"You have date night."

"Yes, but it's not the same. We always talk about the same things and go to the same places."

"You like that, though."

Teresa smiled. "Yes, I do. Now, what about Claudia?"

"I haven't replied to the last email she sent."

"Maybe I should head off so you can do that now. No time like the present."

"I thought you wanted to finish your coffee?"

"I just have. Go and reply. And ring me later and tell me what you said."

As with the first email, it took Izzy a while to compose the words but at least this time, she was happier with what she eventually came up with. The first time, she'd rewritten the email four times before she had the version she read to Teresa and then finally sent. However, this time she only rewrote the text twice.

Hi Claudia

I can't imagine Dad ever saying he'd want nothing to do with you. That's not the sort of person he is. He's upset that he didn't know you existed until now and wishes he could change that. But he'd never tell you to go away.

I've been thinking about the years between when you were born and when you contacted us. What was your childhood like? I spent a lot of time outside, playing with my friends or riding my bike through the pine forest near where we lived. And we never came in until we were called, which was just as it was getting dark. At weekends, we'd go to the beach. On long weekends we'd go camping. What sort of things did you do?

Izzy

Izzy checked the rest of her emails and was about to shut down the computer when she received a reply.

Hi Izzy

I also played outside a lot when I was younger, but what we did changed with the seasons. It's hard to run when you're wearing four layers, a beanie and gloves! On weekends we would go to the country, especially in winter. We have a cabin in the mountains. It's been in our family for three generations. We all love to ski, so we still go to the cabin whenever we can. Do you ski? I first started when I was four. We also spend Christmas at the cabin, a fire going all day, which we need most of all when we come back from our afternoon walk in the snowy forest, necessary even in the cold to walk off the roast lunch.

Claudia

Izzy read the email twice. If Claudia could respond without hesitating, then so could she.

Hi Claudia

Your cabin sounds lovely, especially spending Christmas there. It's nice that it's been in your family for so long. I tried snow skiing once. It was fun, but I wasn't very good at it. I guess it's something you need to try

     <u>The Diary and the Green Dress</u>

a few times before you get the hang of it. I've recently taken up golf which I'm enjoying. It can be frustrating sometimes but also a lot of fun. Do you play any sports?

Izzy

Izzy decided to wait fifteen minutes to see if she received a response. Claudia wrote back in seven.

Hi Izzy

I played a lot of sport when I was younger, but I don't have a lot of spare time between work and family, so now I just play tennis. I would like to try golf one day. Hopefully, when the children are older, I will have some time to try it. My husband Andreas and I have three children, Heidi, Annamarie and Rainer. Are you married?

Claudia

Instead of responding, Izzy turned the computer off and walked away.

Chapter Nine

Have you responded to the last email she sent?

It didn't matter how busy her life was; Teresa rarely forgot anything.

No.

When you do, ask her for a photo.

It's too soon. And she'll want to see one of me.

Then send her one. Aren't you curious to know what she looks like?

Yes, but I'm not ready to know if she looks like me.

You'll find out eventually.

Most of Izzy's photos had other people in them, and she wasn't comfortable sending the ones she did have where she was on her own. In all of the ones by herself, she was too close to the camera. Every detail was clear, from the colour of her eyes to the dimple on her left cheek. Even the shade of the lipstick she was wearing in some of them could be picked easily. Looking at them, she felt exposed, like she was giving away too much of herself too soon. She was about to give up when she remembered Trent had taken one the previous week when they'd gone to Southbank for dinner. She was standing with her back to the Brisbane River with all the city buildings lit up at night, so there was enough in the background that she wasn't the sole focus of the photo.

Hi Claudia

I can't imagine how hard it must be to juggle everything, especially with three children. You must be busy all the time. I don't have any children yet, but I do have a lovely partner named Trent.

I've been wondering a lot lately what you look like. Would you send me a photo? I thought it would be rude to ask and not send one of

 <u>The Diary and the Green Dress</u>

myself, so I've attached a photo to this email. I hope you will send me one in return.

Izzy

Izzy hit the send button before she had time to change her mind. Just as she did, Trent knocked on the door. If he wasn't my partner before, he is now, she said under her breath. Izzy didn't say anything about the email or the photo on the way to her parents' house. She didn't want him to accidentally mention it at dinner in case it upset her mum. Izzy also wasn't sure if she'd done the right thing, no matter what Teresa said. Even though she'd told herself she was ready to see what Claudia looked like, was she? And if Claudia sent one back, should she show it to her mum? As far as Izzy was aware, her mum still didn't know what Claudia looked like. She hadn't wanted to be in the room when the first video call took place, and Izzy doubted she'd been in the room for the ones since. However, a static photo would be easier than a moving, talking person, so maybe she should show her. If she got one back, that is. The more she thought about it, the more she wished something to do with Claudia was straightforward and didn't result in Izzy going back and forth in her head for a long time before deciding what to do.

On the way over to their house, Trent asked some questions about her parents. Partly so he knew something more about them before they met and partly because he wanted to know what to do if the topic of Claudia came up.

"They know I've told you about her, and they're fine with it. They're looking forward to meeting you."

Izzy knew she should have said more, but all she could think about was whether Claudia had seen her photo and if she was going to send one back. Or maybe she already had.

"Come in," Izzy's dad said. "I'm Ben."

Trent shook his hand. "It's nice to meet you."

"Nice to finally meet you too."

Izzy glared at her dad. It wasn't like they'd been going out for six months without Izzy introducing him or that she'd kept him a secret.

"Dinner is almost ready, but we've got time to sit down and have a glass of wine first."

Of course, we do, Izzy thought to herself. She knew her mum would have had dinner ready long before they'd arrived. It was nice though that they were excited to meet Trent. Or maybe they were just happy that so far, he seemed to be a significant improvement on the last man Izzy had introduced to them. A man they included in their family for the eight years after that. Jason had fooled them as well.

"Where's Mum?"

"Here I am. I was just checking things in the kitchen. Hello Trent, I'm Julia."

More likely checking out what Trent looked like from the kitchen, Izzy thought to herself. Ben came back with the wine, and they sat down for longer than either of her parents had planned. The conversation flowed, and it took Izzy to remind her parents that they were supposed to be having dinner.

Even after dinner was served, they kept talking between mouthfuls. Izzy was pleased with how much interest Trent showed in her parents and how he wanted to talk more about them than he did about himself. Jason had always done the opposite. And from the looks on her parents' faces, they were pleased as well. The way the conversation continued, Izzy began to wonder if they'd eventually run out of things to say, but they kept talking until 10 pm when Izzy said they should be going.

On the way home, Trent told her how much he'd enjoyed himself and how much he liked her parents. Before they'd left, out of Trent's hearing, her parents told her how much of an improvement he was on Jason. This one is a keeper, her dad had whispered as they'd headed off. As she looked at him from the corner of her eye, she knew her dad was right. And for the first time, the doubt that had been in the back of her mind started to slip away.

"Do you mind if I look at the diary quickly before I turn the light

     <u>The Diary and the Green Dress</u>

out," Izzy said. "There are only two pages left of this one."

"I'll read it too," Trent said, moving closer to Izzy's side of the bed.

14 July 1921

Lily is nine months old today. Martin still isn't as relaxed around her as he should be. He often picks her up for a minute or two, looks at her closely and then puts her back down, almost as if he's checking she's real. He watches her a lot when she sleeps too. I know he loves her because I can see it in his eyes, and I've heard him say it, although not very often. I've also heard him say he wouldn't be able to forgive himself if something happened to her.

12 August 1921

Lily has a fever. She's had it for weeks now and all I have done, day and night, is keep watch over her. Mother and I took her to the doctor again today. He gave me different medicine this time and said I need to keep her cool to bring her temperature down. I have never felt so helpless. She cries all the time because of the sickness, but I can do nothing to comfort her.

18 August 1921

Lily still has a fever. The doctor came to the house to check on her again. Nothing seems to be working. Martin has been staying away from her. He says he can't get sick because he has to work. I think it's because he doesn't want to see Lily in pain. I wish he wouldn't stay away. Even though Mother has been helping, I wish Martin was here with me. I feel so helpless and sick with worry, and it would comfort me to know that he is also concerned.

20 August 1921

I was up all night with Lily. I gave her a cold bath then took her outside into the night air to see if that would help bring her temperature down, but neither of those things worked. She cried and screamed on and off for hours, and every time she did, it broke another piece of my heart. I can barely stand, but Martin decided to sleep at the factory tonight. He said he had to work very late and start very early so it would be easier to stay there. I am here alone, trying everything I can to help Lily, but noth-ing is working. I can only hope the fever breaks soon.

21 August 1921

Lily died this morning. She was only ten months old.

Chapter Ten

Long after Trent had fallen asleep, Izzy was still staring at the ceiling. Even though they'd talked for a long time about what they'd read, she couldn't put it out of her mind. She turned towards him and watched for a while, the slow deep breaths telling her he wouldn't be waking anytime soon. Eventually, she gave up trying to fall asleep. Rummaging through the trunk, she found the next diary. Unfortunately, there were a lot of gaps between entries.

30 September 1921

I haven't gone anywhere since the funeral. Mother says I need to get out of the house, but I don't want to see anyone. Martin has hardly spoken these past few weeks. He goes to work, comes home, eats dinner in silence and then goes to bed early. I try not to cry in front of him, but sometimes I can't help it. He doesn't say anything when he sees me cry. I wish he would put his arms around me, but he does nothing. So I cry when I'm alone. At least then, I can tell myself he's not comforting me because he can't see me. It sounds silly, but it's what I need to think; otherwise, I have to face the truth—that he doesn't care about Lily or about me. And I can barely think straight as it is. I can't add Martin's coldness to the all-consuming grief I feel.

10 October 1921

All I do is cry. No one else does, including Martin, who I have not seen show any emotion yet. He doesn't say Lily's name either. Doesn't he care? How can he not be grieving our beautiful daughter? He didn't go to work today. He said he was sick, and he stayed in bed all day with the bedroom door shut.

17 October 1921

Martin is still sick. I've never seen him like this before. Mother came to check on him. He was sitting in the front room when she arrived, and he just stared at the wall. When she came out of the room, she looked worried. I could be doing more for Martin, but thoughts of Lily consume my waking hours. The only relief I get is when I'm asleep, and even then, I often dream about her. Last night I dreamt we were walking through a field together. I was holding Lily in my arms, and the late afternoon sun was shining down on us, bathing her in a beautiful light. But then the sun started to set, and the sky became darker. I woke up feeling like I couldn't breathe as tears rolled down my face.

14 November 1921

Today is my brother's birthday. Frank is several years older than me, so we weren't that close growing up, but I have a lot of respect for him now. Susannah has come to see me a few times, and she sat next to me at the dinner table tonight and squeezed my hand from time to time. Thankfully, the children had eaten earlier and weren't at the table. I didn't want to go to the birthday dinner, but Mother said I must. Martin was sick again, so he stayed at home. Whatever he has, it's like no sickness I have seen before. I can't see any symptoms, and when I ask him, he says it's something I wouldn't know about. Part of me wonders if he's feigning sickness so he doesn't have to leave the house and face people. If he won't talk with me about Lily, then he certainly won't want to talk about her with anyone else. As I sat at the dinner table, I thought to myself, if he can stay home, why can't I? I am the one who is openly grieving, and yet I am the one who must remain stoic every time someone comes up to me with their condolences. He should be the one doing that, seeing as he is the one who doesn't seem to care.

15 November 1921

I've spent most of the day in bed. Even though Frank and Susannah's children did not have dinner with us, they came to say goodnight. They looked so happy, and all I could think about was what Lily would have been like at their ages. Martin didn't ask about the dinner, even though he saw I was crying when I got home. I could have tried to hide my tears from him like I have been doing, but I was too upset to care if he saw me or not. It still makes no difference if he sees me, so perhaps I should finally give up hope that he will be there for me one day. That is never going to happen. He slept in the other room and was gone before I woke up. There have been many nights lately when he has slept in the other room, and when he

  <u>The Diary and the Green Dress</u>

has, I've often heard him wake from what I assume are nightmares. I've asked him about them, but he won't say anything. With him already gone, I went back to bed. There was no reason to do anything else. I didn't have the energy anyway, not even to make myself a cup of tea. I only got out of bed again when I heard a knock at the door, and I remembered Bryce had planned to bring a new desk over for Martin. It's the first time I've seen him since Lily's passing, and he told me how sorry he was. As soon as he said it, I started crying. He was kind enough to offer me his handkerchief.

3 January 1922

Christmas passed by in a blur. It should have been Lily's second Christmas. Instead, I watched Frank and Susannah's children open their presents and saw the joy on their faces. Martin and I came home after lunch. I told everyone I was feeling tired and spent the afternoon in bed. I had high hopes for New Year's Eve, but I was disappointed. I thought the ending of one year and the beginning of a new one would give me some respite from my grief. That it would somehow be easier because of the new beginning. But I still grieve as much today as I have every day since she left us. I know I will never forget Lily, but will I get to a point where the grief lessens?

9 January 1922

Martin has changed so much since Lily died, and Mother keeps telling me that I need to look after him. Crying won't bring Lily back, she says. There is nothing you can do for her now, but you can do something for Martin. What can I do for him? He barely speaks to me, so I don't know what to do.

12 January 1922

I haven't seen Martin today. He needed to work late, so he sent Bryce to tell me he would sleep at the factory again. Bryce stayed for a cup of tea, and it was nice to talk to someone instead of sitting by myself with my thoughts.

19 January 1922

I'm worried about Martin. His behaviour has been very strange, stranger than usual. He's slept at the factory almost every night for the past two weeks, and the few times he has come home, he doesn't eat, even though I have cooked him dinner and placed it in front of him. Instead, he sits at the table staring at the food, letting it go cold, before getting up and leaving again. He still hasn't said anything about Lily. I wish he would. He is the only other person who could possibly understand the grief and pain, if he feels anything at all. I think it would help, but if I say her name, he walks away.

14 March 1922

Martin has gone. After weeks of sinking further and further into himself, the doctor has prescribed a rest cure at a facility on the coast. The sea air is supposed to help. These past few months have been so hard. I've grieved for Lily while trying to take care of Martin. I wish someone would take care of me. Mother came after Martin left, and so did Susannah. She brought me a lovely piece of mint green material and some beadwork she had done herself. She thought it might help if I had something to do, something I enjoyed. I spent most of the afternoon sitting in the small room at the back of the house, crying. When I finally ran out of tears, I picked up the fabric. It might be good for me to make a dress from the material—something beautiful. There have not been many beautiful things lately.

21 March 1922

It's been a week since Martin went away. When the doctor came to get him, he said Martin just needed some rest and that he'd make a full recovery. I'm not sure if he's lying to me to spare my feelings or whether he's right. Either way, I have no choice but to wait. The doctor also said I should visit as much as possible as it would help Martin, but to wait for a week or so to make sure Martin had settled in. Father said he would get Bryce to drive me. He also said Bryce would fix anything around the house until Martin comes back.

26 March 1922

Today was the first visit since Martin went to the rest home. He told me he was comfortable and that each day he talked with the doctor. He also said that he was encouraged to go for a walk every day. The rest of the time, we looked at the ocean in silence. There is a bench under a tree near the boundary. The home is on a hill, with a view of the ocean and

 The Diary and the Green Dress

lovely sea breezes.

2 April 1922

I think about Lily more than I think about Martin. I don't tell anyone this. Mother keeps telling me that while it's natural to grieve, I also need to move on with my life and focus on helping Martin get better. The doctor says his mind is not well because of the things he saw during the war. I already know that. What I want to know is how are they going to fix him? And why won't he talk about Lily?

6 April 1922

I have been lost since Lily died. I thought Martin being away would make me feel even more so, but strangely it doesn't. Mother said I need to keep myself busy. I know she means well, but keeping busy won't mend my heart. Today I went to the hospital where she volunteers, not because I wanted to go but because I wanted Mother to stop asking me. I don't think I was much use as Mother's form of volunteering is to sit and talk with the patients, and I didn't feel like talking. And I told her that I would not go into the maternity ward. I wouldn't go into the ward where the returned soldiers are either. Speaking to one of them may have given me some idea of why Martin is the way he is, but I've tried so many times to get him to tell me that I'm not sure I want to know anymore.

Izzy turned the page, but there were no more entries. She leaned back against the wall, her legs still crossed beneath her on the timber floor and looked up at the clock. It was 1 am, long after the time she should have been asleep. But she still wasn't tired, the words Grace had written running through her mind, refusing to be silenced. So she walked out onto the verandah and looked at the city lights. If Grace had stood in the same spot, what had she seen? Not the skyscrapers and city lights that Izzy could see, but what had she looked out on? And had the view given her any peace, the kind of peace Izzy was looking for to quieten her mind so she could go to bed. It took longer than she'd hoped before she started to yawn, her thoughts still consumed by a person she'd never met and who probably died before Izzy was born. Or before Claudia was born.

On her way back to bed, she walked by the office and saw her computer. She hesitated before switching it on. Claudia's email was at the top of the list. Izzy opened the photo before she read the email and then closed it immediately. The same hazel eyes, the same petite nose and dimple on the left cheek. Even her hair was only a shade darker than Izzy's. Of course, they weren't identical, but anyone who saw them would know they were sisters.

Chapter Eleven

The following night, Izzy sat in her car on the driveway, watching the clock on the dashboard tick over while taking several deep breaths. Eventually, she got out, shut the door as quietly as possible and walked slowly to her parents' front door. She didn't get a chance to knock before the door opened. Her dad hugged her; a bit longer than he usually did.

"Does Mum want to see the photo?"

"She's changed her mind five times, but the last thing she said was she'd rather see it with the two of us than on her own."

While her dad went upstairs to find her mum, Izzy opened the email with the photo attached. She stared at Claudia for the seventh time since she'd received the photo, still finding it hard to believe that on the other side of the world, there was a person who looked just like her. And had been there for all the thirty-eight years of Izzy's life.

"Are you both ready?" Izzy asked when her parents came back.

"Yes, we're ready," her dad said.

"Are you sure, Mum?"

Izzy's mum nodded.

No one said anything for a few minutes, and then it was Izzy's mum who spoke first.

"I always wondered that if I'd been lucky enough to have another child, what that child would look like. Seeing as you and Claudia both take after your father, I guess I now know."

Izzy's mum took one last look and then got up.

"Nobody needs to follow me. I just want to be on my own."

Izzy's dad watched her, unsure of whether to go or not. Izzy turned to him and shook her head.

"I know I've seen her a few times now on our video calls, but I still can't believe how similar you both are," he said.

"Neither could I. Are you okay?"

He didn't respond for a few minutes, his eyes not leaving the photo. Then he began to talk about what it was like finding out after all these years. The sadness when he thought about how much he'd missed, the brief moments of anger that he hadn't been able to stop, and the thought that Claudia might have grown up thinking that he hadn't wanted to be part of her life. If he'd known, he would have done all he could to find her.

"I hope that last part didn't upset you."

Izzy shook her head. "Of course you would have tried. She's your daughter."

Izzy thought about the conversation all the way home, wishing she hadn't lied but knowing she had no other choice. She still wasn't ready to share her dad with anyone. But what else could she say? His feelings were a lot more complicated than her own, and she wouldn't forgive herself if she added to what he was dealing with.

After she got home, she'd tried watching TV, ironing the pile of clothes that were in the basket, and having a long conversation with Trent. He offered to come over, but she said no, knowing she wouldn't be good company. After she hung up, she went back to the movie she'd started watching but turned it off after ten minutes. She walked from room to room, looking for something to distract her from thinking about Claudia, her dad, her mum and the whole situation. With nothing else to do, she picked up another diary and stared at the cover for a while before opening it. It wasn't that she'd lost interest. She just wasn't sure she was in the right frame of mind to read about Grace's troubles. But eventually, she decided it was better than thinking about her own.

10 April 1922

I went to the hospital today. Seeing all those people, some much worse than others, made me realise that I am not the only one who has had a terrible thing happen to them. It did not, in any way, make my grief any less, but maybe I could do something to help those people, even if it's a friendly word or bringing someone a cup of tea.

15 April 1922

I spoke with the matron today. She was having a short break when I went in to make a cup of tea for one of the patients. She's older than I am, maybe by fifteen years. She was a nurse during the war, and whenever she gets the chance, she talks with the returned soldiers. Apart from each other, she is the only one who understands what they went through. I don't think she knows about Martin. I haven't said anything, and Mother wouldn't. Talking about someone with a physical injury is one thing, but Martin's injury isn't visible, and no one wants to talk about that.

19 April 1922

Bryce picked me up this morning to take me to see Martin. He's become comfortable talking with me again. The last time he drove me to see Martin, he hardly spoke. It's almost an hour drive, and the time passes more pleasantly now that we are talking as we had previously. There are only so many times you can look at the scenery.

Martin wasn't very talkative today. When I look at him, it's almost as if he isn't there. We sat on the same bench, and he spent most of the time staring out to sea except for one moment when there was a noise in the distance, and he jumped. I asked him what was wrong, and he said nothing. It was hard being there with him, and I was glad of Bryce's company on the way home.

27 April 1922

Another visit with Martin today. He didn't seem to want me there. On the way home, I asked Bryce to stop at the cemetery. It was the first time since the funeral I have been able to bring myself to go. Bryce asked me if I wanted him to stay in the car, but I said no. It brought me comfort to know someone was standing beside me as I looked at her tiny grave and read the words on the headstone.

29 April 1922

Bryce came over to the house today. There was a window that needed fixing. I'm sure I could have tried myself, but Father said he would send Bryce. He and Mother have tried to get me to stay with them while Martin is away, but I won't. Even though I grew up in that house, this one now feels like my home. There are reminders of Lily too. I've packed all her clothes away, but her cot is still in her room. I sometimes walk in and touch it. To take my mind off things, Frank and Susannah invited me to a dance. Because they'll be my chaperones, Mother and Father are happy for me to go. Mother even helped me sew a new dress. I used the mint green material Susannah gave me and added some beading around the neckline, the hem and the ends of the sleeves. It looks so beautiful, and I can't wait to wear it to the dance. Susannah was right that focusing on something nice would help. Bryce said Father asked him to drive me to Frank and Susannah's house. I told him I'm sure Frank wouldn't mind picking me up, but he said it wasn't a bother, and he was happy to do it.

30 April 1922

The dance was wonderful, and I enjoyed it more than I thought I would. The dress looked beautiful, and I received a lot of compliments. Talking to people was hard, though. Everyone knows about Lily and Martin, but no one mentioned them. It was like neither of them had ever existed. On the way home, I sat in the front of the car for the first time because I didn't want Bryce to feel like a chauffeur. He didn't say anything about that, but out of the corner of my eye, I saw him smile. He said I looked lovely in my dress.

Izzy smiled when she read about Grace wearing the dress. She put the diary down and texted Teresa.

I'm glad she wore it somewhere nice.

Me too.

And now we know how old the dress is!

     The Diary and the Green Dress

I can't believe it's lasted so long!

You'll have to get it mended and wear it now.

I know, but I still can't think of somewhere that would warrant a dress like that.

I'm sure Trent will think of something.

After putting her phone down, Izzy walked into her room and pulled the dress out of the wardrobe. She held it up against herself and looked in the mirror, trying to think of an occasion where she could wear it and not be overdressed. There had been plenty of events she'd gone to with Jason where she could have worn it. But if she'd put it on, he would have told her to change into something else, that it was too old fashioned and that she would stand out in the crowd too much. The only one who had been allowed to stand out was him. Hers was a supporting role, doing what she could to make him look good. She was still staring at the dress in the mirror when her phone rang. Probably Teresa, she thought, ringing to talk about the dress. But as she picked up the phone, she saw her parents' number. She answered, and her mum said they needed to see her, so she told them to come to her house the following night. When she mentioned inviting Trent, as with tonight, her parents asked if it could just be the three of them. All the next day, Izzy speculated about what had happened in the few hours between dinner the previous night and the phone call.

"Dinner smells good," her mum said. Apart from hello, it was the first thing either of her parents had spoken since they'd arrived.

"Another half an hour in the oven, and it will be ready."

Her dad poured them all a glass of wine from the bottle he'd brought, and they went out to the verandah.

"So, what's happened?" Izzy said. "Is it something to do with last night?"

Her dad shook his head. "It's not about the photo."

Izzy looked from one to the other. "But I assume it's about Claudia."

This time her dad nodded. "Claudia emailed me asking if it would be ok with us if she came to Brisbane to meet us."

Izzy looked at her mum, but she just kept staring at the view.

"She mentioned something to me in one of her emails about meeting one day."

"She was more specific in the email she sent me," her dad said. "She wants to meet us this year."

"What? When?" Izzy said.

"She didn't give a specific date. She just said she wanted it to be this year."

Her mum stood up and said she was going to check the oven. And there was no more discussion about Claudia that night. Even though Izzy had tried to bring up the proposed visit again, her mum changed the subject. The prospect of the visit had been raised, and as far as Julia was concerned, that was all that needed to be said for now.

After her parents left, Izzy turned her attention to packing. Trent had organised a long weekend in the Sunshine Coast Hinterland and would be picking her up first thing in the morning. She hadn't been on a weekend away with a man since Jason. He'd loved going away for the weekend, always in the fanciest hotels with the best restaurants. Thinking about it now, Izzy realised it had been more about him being able to tell people where he'd been and what he'd done rather than spending time with her. A weekend away with someone who was thinking about her, rather than themself, would be a nice change. If only she could stop thinking about Claudia.

"I've brought some supplies," Trent said as he put her bag in the boot of his car the next morning. "Just some nibbles and wine. There's a creek that runs next to the verandah of our cabin, and I thought it would be nice to sit out there in the afternoon."

As they drove up the highway, Trent shared with Izzy what he had researched about the area where they were going to stay. And about all the things they could do. He'd even researched the best restaurants in the areas around where they were staying.

     <u>The Diary and the Green Dress</u>

"There are a few excellent bushwalks nearby, so I hope you packed your walking shoes."

"Yes, I did," Izzy replied, although she wasn't the biggest fan of bushwalking.

The last time she'd gone, she ended up with a leech on her leg, and there had been a snake sunning itself in the middle of the path. Hopefully, this would be a very different experience.

With only one wrong turn, they arrived at their destination. Whatever misgivings Izzy had earlier about spending three whole days together went straight out the window. It was beautiful—the cabin, the surroundings, the view. There was no way that anything other than having a wonderful long weekend could happen here. As soon as she walked into the cabin and saw the fireplace, the large spa bath and the view of the bush from the windows, she forgot all about Claudia, and the photo, and the visit.

"What do you think?" Trent asked.

"It's fantastic."

"Glad you like it. I know you've had a lot on your mind lately, so I don't want you thinking about anything. Instead, what I want you to do is go and sit outside on the deck."

Ten minutes later, Trent came out with a platter covered in cheeses, olives, sun-dried tomatoes, dolmades, salami and prosciutto—all the things that Izzy loved. The platter was accompanied by a bottle of French champagne.

"There's a lot of food, but we didn't have lunch, so I thought you might be hungry."

Izzy watched as he poured two glasses. She still wasn't used to someone being so considerate. She could easily get used to it.

They sat outside on the verandah for the next two hours, just talking, eating, and sipping champagne while watching the creek flow by their cabin. Izzy felt relaxed for the first time in ages, and even though it was only the first day, she already wished they were staying longer.

The following morning, Trent cooked breakfast and then pulled out the map of the walking trails he'd picked up at reception.

"This walk looks good. There's a waterfall at the end. Shall we try it?"

Izzy nodded. "But if I see a snake, I'll be on your shoulders within a second."

Trent laughed. "It's winter. The snakes will be hibernating."

"I don't care if it's winter. It only takes one snake to forget what season it is and come out in the open."

"I promise I will keep the snakes away from you."

True to his word, Trent walked beside her, held her hand, and kept an eye out for snakes. Izzy found herself enjoying the walk more than she thought she would. The scenery was beautiful, the walking trail cutting through a rainforest with trees of all shapes and sizes, lush and green all the way to the canopy and on the ground, not a spot of bare earth to be seen with plants covering the rainforest floor. It was such a contrast to some of the areas they'd seen on the drive up, the ground in those places hard and brown, a sign that drought was never far away. But here, it felt like water was captured in the cool, fresh air. And the waterfall at the end was worth every step they'd taken. Crystal clear blue water cascaded over the rocks above. It plunged onto the edge of a deep pool at the bottom before flowing out in ripples to the shore. Izzy put her hand in the water, but it was freezing.

"I wish it was summer and we could go swimming."

Trent nodded. "Maybe we could come back in summer."

Izzy looked at him out of the corner of her eye, her head still turned towards the waterfall. Summer was still a few months away, but Trent seemed happy to include her in those months ahead. It was a change she was still getting used to. But one that she found easier with each day.

As they walked back to the car park, Izzy took photos of the sunlight as the rays broke through the trees. Even though there were so many trees blocking the sun from getting all the way through, it still managed to shine amid the cool darkness, highlighting the colours of the rainforest.

     The Diary and the Green Dress

After the walk, Trent suggested they drive down to the nearest village, which was Montville. Even though he didn't refer to anything before he suggested it, she knew it was one of the things on the to-do list while they were there, the list she was sure he was mentally ticking off. She hadn't asked him how much time he'd spent researching, but she appreciated the effort he'd gone to.

The village itself was quaint, with lots of small shops along the main street selling everything from cuckoo clocks to fudge, but there were a lot of people around. From the conversations she overheard, most of them had come up from Brisbane for the weekend as Izzy and Trent had done. She also heard several other languages, and Izzy wondered how tourists from other countries had found this village in the hinterland, an hour and a half's drive north of the airport they'd likely landed at. As she watched them all walking back and forth, ducking into the shops and coming out with bags filled with trinkets and souvenirs, she wondered how those items would look when the tourists got them back to their city homes. Would those items be a reminder of their time here, or would they end up in a drawer, the owners wondering how they had got carried away and bought things they didn't need and would never use? Usually, Izzy would have liked to explore the street and see what was down the alleyways, but the bustle of the street wasn't what she wanted, and she decided she'd rather be back in a place where it was just the two of them.

"How about lunch before we head back?" Trent said. "According to the reviews, there's a great pub just down the road. It's on my list of things to do while we're here."

Izzy smiled. She'd been right about him mentally ticking items off the list. He really had gone to a lot of trouble to make sure she had a lovely weekend away. So, she changed her mind and agreed to stay a bit longer.

After they'd finished eating, they both looked down at their plates, and Izzy wondered whether agreeing to stay for lunch had been the right decision. The meals were so big that it didn't look like they'd touched them, even though they were both full. Looking around them, it seemed like they weren't the only ones having the same problem. If Izzy and Trent had or-dered the same meals at one of the restaurants they usually went to, it would have been half the size but twice the price. Here, it was like the owners didn't want anyone to leave hungry. Either that or they were trying to fatten up the tourists. When the waiter came to get their plates, Izzy said how delicious their meals had been, not wanting him to think that they didn't like them because there was so much left. But he said most people couldn't eat everything they'd been served, and he would package the leftovers up for them. They already had more food than they could eat back at the cabin, but they said they'd take the leftovers anyway. From the look on Trent's face, she could tell he was mentally going through all the food he'd brought, trying to figure out if they could fit the leftovers in somewhere. Izzy reached over, took his hand and thanked him again for putting so much effort into the weekend. Neither of them was in a hurry to move until their stomachs had settled, so they stayed at their table a while longer. As Izzy observed the other patrons again, she noticed a family in the corner that hadn't been there when she'd been checking out the size of everyone's meal. The couple looked to be in their early forties, and the three children were all about primary school age. They were laughing and talking, and it wasn't until the father walked by Izzy and Trent's table with his son that she heard them speak. And they were talking to each other in German. Sometime this year, if the plans went ahead, another German couple with three children would be landing at the same airport this family likely had. Izzy closed her eyes for a second and then told Trent she'd be more comfortable back at the cabin. At least then, she could lie down until she didn't feel so full. Or so conflicted.

On the drive back, it started to rain. That put a stop to any more bushwalks that day, for which Izzy said a silent thank you, even though after the lunch they'd had, another walk was probably a good idea. Although she'd enjoyed the morning walk, it hadn't turned her from someone used to walking on concrete to someone who wanted to spend every spare minute in nature. There are too many creatures for her liking, the memory of the leech from the last time still fresh in her mind. One bushwalk a day was enough. She didn't want to push her luck. The following day was soon enough for another walk. In the meantime, the rain gave them an excuse to use the spa bath after their lunch had settled. Izzy didn't mention the family in the corner. Trent didn't either, but then he might not have seen or heard them. Or maybe he had and didn't say anything because Izzy had yet to mention how she felt about the possible visit.

"Our dinner reservation isn't until 7.30 pm, so we've got a few hours before we have to head out again," Trent said later that afternoon as he lit a fire.

"Thank goodness for that. I'm going to need another few hours before I even think about food again."

If Trent hadn't been talking about the restaurant they were going to and how much he was looking forward to it, she would have suggested they stay in and eat the leftovers for dinner. But he'd been telling her about it since he'd booked the weekend away, so while she was content to stay by the fire and not venture out, she would put on the dress she packed and head out in time for their reservation.

"How about I pour us a glass of wine then? The rest of the nibbles can wait until tomorrow."

"Sounds good. I've brought the latest diary with me. We can sit in front of the fire and read a few pages."

"You grab the diary; I'll grab the wine."

5 May 1922

I've just come back from visiting Martin. He mentioned Lily for the first time, only briefly. All he said was, 'Lily, I wish I could have…', and then he stopped. I asked him what he was going to say next, but he wouldn't say anymore. So, we sat in silence for the rest of the visit. When I came home, Mother called around and asked how he was. I told her what he said, and she was quiet for a moment and then said, 'I'm sure he'll be back soon.' I'm not so sure about that. He doesn't seem to be getting any better at all. When I spoke with Dr Morrison, he said Martin was doing well, but I think he was just sparing my feelings, as I know he's done on previous occasions. I think he believes I won't be able to handle the truth. Everyone thinks I'm so delicate, and maybe I was before Lily. But not anymore. I cannot survive by being delicate.

6 May 1922

Yesterday's visit with Martin has left me feeling drained, and I was tired after the long drive, so tired that I can't even be bothered to write anything else down. At least having Bryce to keep me company made the journey more enjoyable.

12 May 1922

I cried in the car today. I didn't want to, but I couldn't stop. Martin just stared out to sea the whole time I was there and barely acknowledged that I'd come to see him, that I'm trying to do all that I can to help him get better. I'm alone when I'm at home, and I'm alone when I'm with my husband. Bryce asked if there was anything he could do. I said no, but it was nice that someone asked. He's been helping with things around the house, and that is enough. Mother is worried that people will talk about another man being in the house while Martin is away. I'm sure some of them will. You can't stop people like that. But most people who know me also know that Bryce works for my father. The times he is there are the only times I don't feel alone in the house.

15 May 1922

Mother came by today to take me out. She's involved in fundraising for a statue to honour the fallen. The fundraising meeting went for two hours, although most of the first hour was spent drinking tea and gossiping. For a lot of Mother's friends, gossiping is their favourite pastime. I'm glad Mother didn't join in. There were many glances in my direction, and I think they were meant to be subtle, but they weren't. I wondered if they usually gossiped about me out of Mother's earshot. It would be an exciting story for them—a husband who isn't quite right and had to be sent away and a child who was taken far too soon. They probably think I'm cursed. Or they probably blame me. The latter is more likely. I've grown up around them, and I know how they think. At least by the end of the meeting, there was a plan for raising the money.

As I walked out the door, I couldn't help but wonder what Martin's reaction to the statue would be. Bryce drove us home after the meeting. He drove to my parents' house first, which he doesn't usually do. Mother doesn't think it looks right if Bryce takes me home last, but she had to be home at a specific time. We talked after Mother had gone, and it was nice to talk about everyday things. Before he left, we arranged a time for him to drive me out to see Martin tomorrow. I'm glad it's Bryce driving me.

     The Diary and the Green Dress

He hasn't seemed uncomfortable doing that and waiting for me until I'm ready to go. I can't think of anyone else I know who would do that.

16 May 1922

Visiting Martin is difficult, and sometimes I don't want to go. It's a depressing place, and I feel sad when I see some of the men there. I think some will never leave. I'm still not sure if Martin wants me to visit. I talk more with Bryce on the way there and back than I do during the actual visit with Martin. Bryce and I talk about many things, which surprises me, considering the different worlds we come from. I don't know anything about life on a farm, so I ask him a lot of questions. I ask a lot of questions about his family too. From the things he says, they sound like very nice people and all very close. I keep thinking about how different my life would be if I'd married someone like Bryce rather than someone like Martin.

"Getting married is a big commitment," Trent said. "You want to be sure before making that commitment with someone. I only plan on getting married once."

Izzy nodded, pushing Jason to the back of her mind. "So do I."

"I'm glad we're on the same page. I'm enjoying being with you, Izzy. It's taken me a long time to find someone I love."

Trent kissed her and then got up to rinse out their wine glasses. For the first time, she felt nothing but happiness at hearing him say those words.

Chapter Twelve

"How was the long weekend?"

Izzy hadn't even unpacked her bag when Teresa rang. It must have taken all her self-control to wait until now to call. It wouldn't have surprised Izzy if Teresa had texted her over the weekend to check how things were going.

"It was good."

"Just good."

Izzy laughed. "You're very curious, aren't you?"

"Of course I am. You spent three whole days together. If it went well, then it's a great sign."

"A great sign for what?"

"That you'll be able to live together."

"Slow down a minute. It was just a long weekend."

"It's never just a long weekend. And besides, you're in love now."

Izzy smiled to herself. Yes, she was.

"So, did you get on well the whole time?" Teresa asked. "Did Trent enjoy it?"

Izzy gave her a quick rundown on the weekend. Not everything, though. As glad as she was that Teresa was happy for her, she didn't need to know all the details of her relationship with Trent. Especially as they worked in the same office.

"It sounds like a perfect weekend. You'll be moving in together before you know it."

"We'll see. I'm in no hurry to do that anytime soon."

"You can't put it off forever."

"Maybe not, but it will be a while before we even talk about something like that."

After she hung up, Izzy thought about what Teresa had said. Izzy knew that Teresa only wanted the best for her but did that equal living with someone? She'd done that before, and it hadn't worked out so well. Did she want to rush into that again? As much as she'd enjoyed the weekend, Izzy was glad she was by herself that night. She finished unpacking and then looked at the clock. She had to get up early in the morning for a working breakfast, but the diary she'd taken on the weekend was the last thing she'd pulled out of the bag, and there were only a few pages left.

1 June 1922

I just got word from Dr Morrison that Martin had some sort of setback and that he'll have to stay for a few more months. Even though no one says anything to my face, I know people are talking about him. I don't discuss his condition with his parents. I don't know if they talk privately to one another, but they've never said anything to me. I know they care about him because they're a very close family, but, like mine, there are some things you don't talk about. They haven't mentioned Lily since the funeral either. I don't know whether they're trying to protect my feelings by not talking about her or whether it hurts them to talk about her, but I wish they would. I wish someone would. When no one mentions her, it's like she never existed. But she did, and she was beautiful. She was my angel.

10 June 1922

Another visit with Martin today. Dr Morrison stopped me on the way in and asked me to come to his office. He wanted to talk to me about a delicate subject, which he was too embarrassed to talk about directly, but I could pick up his meaning. He thinks it would be good for Martin if we were intimate. Physical touch might help, he said. Even though I didn't want to do that, I thought if it would help Martin, then I should. It's still not enjoyable for me, but I guess it's not meant to be. As Mother told me before I got married, it is just something I have to put up with.

22 June 1922

Bryce came to the house today. Another window required fixing. While he was here, he asked me when I needed him to drive me to see Martin again, and I started crying. He put his arm around me while I cried. It felt so comforting.

26 June 1922

Bryce kissed me today. It wasn't planned. It just happened. Maybe Dr Morrison is right and physical contact does help. Bryce left soon after. He was very embarrassed and couldn't stop apologising. He said he would stay away from me if I felt uncomfortable. I told him I didn't feel uncomfortable and could have pulled away, but I didn't. The truth is, I enjoyed it much more than when Martin kisses me.

28 June 1922

It happened again today. Bryce drove me to the grocery store, and after he helped me carry the groceries inside, as we stood in the kitchen, he kissed me. For those few moments when we kissed, I felt happy and all the bad things that have happened disappeared, just for a minute. While he was looking at me, I didn't turn away but looked straight at him. He has beautiful eyes, and when he smiles, his whole face lights up. It's nice to see him smile. I can't remember the last time I saw Martin smile.

8 July 1922

We stopped at Bryce's house on the way home from visiting Martin. He had to pick up some tools to repair a loose board on the verandah. It came loose yesterday, and I tripped over it, so Bryce said he would fix it straight away. I followed him inside because I wanted to see where he lived. If someone had seen me, it would have got back to Mother and Father, and I would never hear the end of it. What did I think they'd say? You know how people talk. Yes, I know how people talk, but Bryce lives on the city's outskirts, and there is no one else around. Besides, I just wanted to see what his house was like and from what I saw, it could use a woman's touch.

9 July 1922

> *I gave it a lot of thought before writing this next entry, but once I found the key to lock the drawer in my desk, I knew I had a safe place to hide my diary. I've been truthful about other events in my life that I have recorded here, and this should be no different. After Bryce fixed the board, he needed to go back to the factory for a few hours, and I asked if he would like to come back later for dinner. He arrived at about 8 pm, much later than I usually eat, but he decided to walk because he said he needed some exercise. I wondered afterwards if it was because he didn't want to leave the factory car, which everyone would recognise, outside my house. We ate dinner together but didn't talk very much. It was as if we both suddenly felt shy. I cleaned up the kitchen while Bryce had a glass of whisky. I knew what was going to happen, but I didn't feel nervous. Afterwards, I couldn't believe how different it was with Bryce. I enjoyed it, and I felt things I had never felt before. With Bryce, it didn't feel like something I just had to put up with, and he wanted to make sure I liked it too.*

10 August 1922

> *What I'm doing with Bryce has to stop. I know it's wrong, but it's the only thing in my life that gives me any joy. Martin has made no progress, even though his doctors tell me my visits are doing him good. On the drive back, I keep telling myself that I should ask Bryce to drive me straight home, but I don't. Instead, I sit next to him and hope he drives us to his house.*

Izzy put down the diary and looked at the clock. Teresa always stayed up late. And telling her about Grace and Bryce would distract her from asking any more questions about her and Trent.

"What?" she said. "Say that again."

"Grace and Bryce had sex."

"I knew they'd end up having an affair. You need to start reading the next diary and find out what happens."

"You'll be the first person I tell."

"So I should be."

Izzy laughed, and then they talked for the next twenty minutes about Grace and Bryce. How long did their affair go on? Did anyone ever find out? Did they mostly go to Bryce's house because it was out of the way? So many things they wanted to know. But what they both liked about what Izzy had read was that Grace seemed to be happy for the first time in a long time. Even though what Grace was doing was wrong. And if Martin ever found out, it would feel like a knife had been plunged into his heart and slowly twisted. At least that's what it had felt like for Izzy. No matter how much time passed, she still remembered exactly what she'd felt like when she'd found out. Not just the feeling of a knife in her heart, but the lethargy, which was so strong that even lying on her bed staring out the window at the sky, had taken more energy than she had to give. The wasted hours she'd wandered around the house, telling herself that the next day would be better, that the next day she'd achieve something. But when the next day came, she found herself lying down, staring out the window again. It had been like that for the first three weeks until one day, she picked herself up and said enough was enough. She'd moved out a few days later.

"Before I go, I forgot to ask earlier. What's happening with Claudia? Any more news about her meeting you?"

The news about Grace and Bryce had stopped her from asking any more about Trent, but it hadn't distracted her from the other significant change in Izzy's life. At least it would stop her mind and her heart remembering what the metaphorical knife had felt like.

"There was an email when I got home this afternoon. She sent it to dad and me. She's thinking of coming to Brisbane during the Christmas holidays."

"Wow, that's big. Do you think Claudia will come?"

"I think so."

"Where will she stay? At a hotel? Or with you? Or your parents?"

Izzy hadn't thought about that. She was still getting used to the idea that what had started out as a notion that one day they'd meet now seemed to be turning into actual plans to meet. In the same country. The same city. The same room. Standing across from each other.

     <u>The Diary and the Green Dress</u>

"She didn't say, but surely she'll book a hotel room. She's never met us before, and if it doesn't go well, it would be uncomfortable for everyone if she was staying with one of us. Besides, I don't think mum is ready for that."

"You think it might not go well?"

"I don't know. I hope it does, but I won't know until Claudia gets here."

Izzy thought about it as she lay in bed. As much as she hoped things would go well, there was no way she could be sure. Any number of things could go wrong. Claudia might be so different from all of them that they didn't get along. She might not be truthful in the emails she was sending, and she actually was angry at their dad for not being there for her. Their dad. She still struggled to say it, and every time those words went through her head, they made her catch her breath.

Chapter Thirteen

Three nights later, the phone rang. Izzy looked at the time. It was 11.30 pm.

"Who's ringing at this time of night?" Trent said.

Izzy shrugged. She didn't recognise the number and wasn't going to answer, but something changed her mind.

"Hello, is this Isabel?"

The German accent immediately let her know who it was.

"Claudia?"

"Yes. Hello."

And with those two words, Isabel could no longer deny that Claudia was real.

"Hi Claudia. Yes, it's Isabel."

"It's nice to finally talk to you."

"It's nice to talk to you too. And a little strange, I must admit."

"Yes, it is. But I knew from the first time our father mentioned you I'd want to get to know you."

Seeing it written was one thing. Hearing Claudia say it was something else entirely, and she didn't speak for a few moments.

"I hope I didn't upset you by saying that. It must be very strange for you to hear me say it."

"No, you didn't upset me. It's just that until now, I thought I was an only child. I never thought I would hear anyone refer to Dad as our father."

"No, I'm sure you didn't."

"I've enjoyed reading your emails."

"I've enjoyed reading yours too. I rang because I wanted to let you know about our plans for Christmas."

Izzy held the phone a little bit tighter. There was no more doubt. The visit was happening.

"I'll be coming with my husband Andreas and our children, Heidi, thirteen, Annamarie, eleven and Rainer, eight. All the children talk about lately is wanting to go to Australia and learning to surf."

Izzy forced herself to laugh. "As long as I don't have to be involved in teaching them. Surfing is something I've never mastered."

Claudia laughed as well. Izzy could tell it wasn't forced. "I'm not going to be involved either. I can't imagine trying to stand up on a surfboard. They're excited about the time of year as well. They've never had a summer Christmas."

"Just be warned that it gets very hot and humid."

"It will be a nice change from the cold. Also, it's a quiet time at work for me. I travel a lot but not around Christmas."

Izzy realised in all the communications so far, Claudia hadn't mentioned what her job was.

"What do you do for work?"

"I'm an architect. I mainly work on large commercial projects, which is why I have to travel."

"Sounds like you have an interesting job. Where do you travel to?"

"London mostly. The company I work for has an office there. Sometimes I go to other countries in Europe like France and Spain. It just depends on where the next project is."

That explains why Claudia speaks English so well, Izzy thought. London was another place she hadn't been to but would like to see. They talked for another ten minutes before Claudia had to head to a meeting with a client. Izzy hung up and went outside onto the verandah and looked at the night sky. It was a beautiful, clear night, and there was a full moon. It was daytime where Claudia was. Izzy wondered if she'd rung from her office or if she'd walked outside. If she had rung from her office, did she shut the door so no one could hear the conversation? And had Claudia thought about what she was going to say before she rang?

"Are you all right?" Trent asked as he came and stood beside her.

Izzy nodded and told him about the conversation. "It was just strange hearing her voice."

"Will you be okay meeting them at Christmas?"

"I have to be. They're all coming."

Izzy looked up at the moon. Had Claudia ever looked up at the night sky and thought about her family on the other side of the world?

"We should go back to bed."

It was late, and Izzy knew he was right, but she couldn't sleep. Again. Claudia's laugh sounded too much like her own. And from the sounds of it, she was very successful. A high-powered career, a family, a cabin in the woods. She lay there until 2 am and then got up. The diaries had been there for her on many other nights; there was no reason this one should be any different. She sighed as she picked it up. She'd rather be asleep. When would this feeling leave?

3 September 1922

I've been too distracted lately to write in my diary. For the past three weeks, I've felt sick in the mornings, and I know what that means. I should have stopped what I was doing with Bryce. I should never have started in the first place. When it becomes apparent, I'll have to find a way to hint at the intimate visits with Martin. Even though there have only been two. What have I done? What if Martin isn't the father?

Izzy shut the diary. It hadn't been the distraction she'd hoped for. She hopped back into bed, and Trent didn't stir, not even when she sat up

     The Diary and the Green Dress

and reached for a tissue to wipe away the tears. Why couldn't people be happy with the person they were committed to, married or not? It was a long time before she fell asleep, something Teresa picked up on during their conversation the next morning. Izzy's constant yawning gave it away.

"I'll be over straight after work," Teresa said. "And Trent isn't Jason."

She'd needed to talk to someone about the visit, and while Trent had been full of practical suggestions of what to do when they arrived, she needed to speak to someone about how she felt. About Claudia and about the feelings that had come up after she'd read the diary entry. Trent was good at black and white and trying to solve anything that cropped up. But the situation with Claudia wasn't black and white. It was very grey. And sometimes, Izzy couldn't find the words to accurately explain what was going through her mind. Trent found that hard because he wanted to fix the situation, even though she didn't need him to fix anything. She just needed to talk about what was going on. To try and get it straight in her head. And the feelings from last night, that wasn't something she wanted to talk to Trent about. So far, she'd said very little about her previous relationship, and she wasn't in a hurry to change that.

"So Christmas it is," Teresa said as she walked in the door.

Izzy nodded.

"You'll have to buy them presents."

Izzy groaned. "I hadn't thought of that. What on earth would I buy? I don't know them yet."

"You've got time to figure it out. Plus, you'll need to decide how much time you'll spend with them."

How much time they'd spend together hadn't crossed Izzy's mind, something Teresa could tell by the look on her face.

"One step at a time. Tell me what the rest of the family looks like."

Izzy shrugged.

"Haven't you looked her up on social media yet?"

Izzy shook her head.

"Why not? What are you waiting for?"

Izzy picked up her phone and searched for Claudia. The settings on her account were private, but she could see her profile photo and surrounding her were a man and three children. They both looked closely at the photo. It seemed Andreas didn't get much of a look in. The children were a carbon copy of Claudia. As Izzy stared at the family in front of her, she realised that if anyone saw the children with Izzy, they would pass as her own. And just for a moment, Izzy let herself think that it was her in the photo. That Jason never cheated, and they were the ones smiling at the camera, children on either side. Another thing he'd said he wanted. Another lie. She lowered her phone and waited until the pain slid away.

"They're two very different people," Teresa said, squeezing her hand. "Nothing like each other. And besides, who's to say you won't have a similar photo at some point."

Izzy nodded. Teresa was right. And she was happier with Trent than she'd ever been with Jason. She had to try harder to let go of the thoughts of what might have been if Jason hadn't been who he was and focus on the life she actually had. One that wasn't based on lies. A life with someone clear about who he was. She turned towards Teresa, who was still holding her hand and thanked her for the reminder.

"Any time," she said smiling before glancing down at the diary that was sitting on the coffee table.

Izzy picked it up and handed it to her.

"We can keep talking if you want to," Teresa said.

Izzy shook her head. "I'm okay. Flick through the pages until you find an entry that tells us something about the situation Grace found herself in."

10 September 1922

I told Martin today. I wasn't ready to tell him, but I was sick during my visit. He didn't say anything, and I was glad about that. I didn't want

    <u>The Diary and the Green Dress</u>

to talk about it. I left soon afterwards. I didn't speak in the car on the way home. Bryce asked if I was all right, and I said I was tired, and I kept my eyes closed for the rest of the journey. I willed myself not to be sick, and I asked him to drive me straight home.

14 September 1922

Mother has been checking on me every day. I think she suspects, but she hasn't said anything. She and Father are still trying to get me to stay at their house. I told her I hadn't changed my mind. I know they'll keep pressuring me, but I'm happier in my own home. Also, if I'm at their house, I will have no opportunity to see Bryce with no one else around. I know I should say something. Eventually, it will be obvious, and he'll wonder. I know he will.

"She has to tell him," Teresa said. "It better be in this diary."

"I'm sure it will be. If not this one, then one of the others. Grace hasn't been shy about writing other things down, and she doesn't seem like the sort of person who would keep something so important from him."

Her friend didn't look convinced. Given the time and circumstances Grace found herself in, maybe Teresa was right, and she was wrong. She hoped not. For Bryce to spend the rest of his life wondering, she couldn't even begin to imagine what that would be like.

Izzy looked down at the diary in Teresa's hands. "I wonder if she changed the place she kept them after she started writing about Bryce. A locked desk drawer isn't very secure."

"She wouldn't need to while Martin was away."

"True, but when he comes back…"

"If he comes back."

"You don't think he does?"

"I don't know. From what we've read so far, he wasn't in a good way."

"Surely, the doctors helped him."

Teresa shrugged. "Maybe. Maybe not. Hopefully, Grace will let us know. In the meantime, I want to find out if she tells Bryce."

Izzy scanned the pages as she turned them but found nothing. She was beginning to think they'd have to start searching through other diaries, and then, on the second last page, they found the entry they were looking for.

11 October 1922

I was sick while Bryce was here, and I told him. He was quiet for a while before asking if it was possible. I wanted to say that after what we'd been doing that of course, it was possible, but the look on his face stopped me, so instead, I just nodded. We sat in silence for a while. Then he asked about Martin. I didn't want to say that was possible too, so I nodded again. He asked how we would know for sure. There was nothing I could say in response. There is no way to know for sure.

Izzy turned to the last page, but it was blank.

"Where's the next one?"

"Still in the trunk. I'll get it."

As she pulled each of the remaining diaries out, she flicked through them, checking the dates.

"It's not here," Izzy called out.

"What do you mean it's not here?" Teresa called back.

"Exactly that. The next diary isn't with the other ones."

"Let me look," Teresa said, coming up behind her.

She flicked through them all, just as Izzy had, but couldn't see the one they wanted.

"What do we do now?"

Izzy shook her head. "I don't know. Let's just think for a minute. It has to be here somewhere."

"Was there anything else in the house when you got here?"

"The shoebox!"

"What shoebox?"

"On the top shelf of the wardrobe in my room. There was an old shoebox pushed to the back. I meant to pull it down when I saw it, but I was in the middle of something else and forgot about it. It's still up there."

They ran down the hall to Izzy's bedroom.

"We'll need a chair," Izzy said.

Teresa turned and ran back down the hallway, picked up a chair from the dining room and ran back. Izzy laughed when she saw the look of excitement on Teresa's face.

"I think you should get the box down."

Izzy hadn't even finished the sentence before Teresa was up on the chair and reaching for the box.

"It's very dusty. Maybe we should take it outside so we don't get dust all over your bedroom floor."

Even amid her excitement, Teresa was still practical. Plus, her house was always spotless, even with Jack and Rosie constantly running around. But Izzy couldn't afford a cleaner like Teresa could, so her house wasn't as spotless. Some dust on the floor at Teresa's would be instantly noticeable. Here it would just blend in with the other dust until the next time Izzy vacuumed. They took the box outside to the verandah anyway, and Teresa lifted the lid.

"Look at those shoes," Izzy said. "They're beautiful."

"And look what's underneath them."

"Shoes always come first. They must have been Grace's. Look at the style."

The shoes were cream with a small, squarish heel, a rounded toe, and a t-strap with some beading similar to what was on the green dress.

"I can't believe you have the complete outfit. I don't care where or when, but you have to wear it."

Izzy held the shoes in her hand. "Too small for me. There's no way my feet would fit into these."

"Ok, just the dress. And the purse. I'll let you get away with not wearing the headband."

Izzy carefully put the shoes down beside the box on the table and then looked back inside. There was a leather notebook. The cover was brown like the diaries, but it was smaller, and the first few pages were filled with notes about things that had needed to be done around the house.

"That's disappointing," Teresa said.

Izzy nodded, putting the notebook down on the table beside her. "I guess we'll never know."

As Izzy picked up the shoes to put back in the box, she bumped the notebook, and it fell on the floor, the back cover falling open. The first thing Izzy could see was a date.

16 May 1923

"I think we've found it."

Teresa looked over Izzy's shoulder, and they both started reading.

Hettie is beautiful. She was born a week ago, and I have been smiling ever since. I can't stop looking at her. She is sleeping beside me as I write this. But, with joy also comes fear. Although I try not to, I can't leave her alone for a minute. I'm afraid of what will happen if I do.

30 May 1923

Mother is very happy. She said it was just what I needed. If only she knew the truth. I know she means well, thinking this will help me get over Lily, but nothing will do that. This baby is not a replacement but another human being. Every time I look at her, I try to see who she looks like, but she is too young for that to be clear. Maybe in a few months, it will be evident, so I will have to wait. I keep praying that she looks like me.

Bryce came by today. I needed to buy some food, so he drove me to the store. Mother was here, and she looked after Hettie while I was gone. It's the first time he has seen Hettie as Father had sent him to Melbourne on factory business. I was worried about what would happen, but Bryce just said how lovely she looked and spoke with Mother for a minute before we left. In the car, he started talking about Hettie, saying how beautiful she was and how he had wanted a child for many years. The odds are in favour of Hettie being his, but there is no way to tell. He wants certainty, and I can't give him that. It was the first time I'd thought about how this is affecting him. For the rest of his life, he will wonder.

"It's almost the opposite of the situation with your dad," Teresa said.

"Yes, dad may have only just found out, but at least there is a certainty. Poor Bryce."

"I've been thinking about your dad and how he must be feeling."

Izzy nodded. "I do that all the time. He's keeping a lot to himself. I think he wants to protect me."

"Of course he does, but you're involved as well. Claudia's your half-sister."

"Who I'm going to meet at Christmas."

"And hopefully, I'll meet her too."

Izzy smiled. "I didn't think there was any chance of Claudia coming without you meeting her at some point."

Teresa laughed. "You're spot on there. Now show me the next entries."

25 June 1923

Because Martin is away longer than initially thought—and that's how everyone refers to it—he's just away, Mother and Father asked Bryce to help out more than he has been. If only they knew. But at least I get to see him. Mother had a meeting at the church this morning. She's organising a fundraising effort for a family who lost their house in a fire. So when Bryce came to take me to the shops, I took Hettie with us. He held the basket she was in but walked behind me. I didn't like that. It made it look like he was my servant, but it's what we have to do when we are in public. I couldn't stop thinking that it was almost like a family outing. Almost, but not quite. He carried the groceries in when we got home and, in the kitchen, he kissed me, and it felt so lovely. He spent a long time looking at Hettie and asked if he could pick her up. It almost broke my heart watching him hold her. It's so unfair. Bryce is here with me, and he cares for me. Martin is not well, and I don't know if he'll ever be well again. Even before he went away, he was distant. I don't know what will happen when he comes back.

30 June 1923

Bryce came by again today. The door from the back verandah to the kitchen won't shut properly, and he came to fix it. Mother was fussing in the kitchen. The way I stack dishes takes up too much room in the cupboard, she said. I just sipped my tea and tried to ignore her, which was easy because I looked at Bryce out of the corner of my eye, hoping I wasn't obvious. He was looking at me too, every time Mother turned away. How I wished she needed to go somewhere.

The thought of stolen moments stayed in her mind long after Teresa left. Izzy understood why they had to act like that, but it must have been hard being in the same room as the person you love and not acknowledging it in any way. Even though she told herself not to think about it, Izzy couldn't help but go back to the night she and Jason had gone to a party at a friend's house. They'd been in the same room, and after a few too many drinks, Jason started telling the host about the affair he was having. Thankfully Izzy had been on the other side of the room and didn't hear him. The thought of finding out at a crowded party was too awful to think about. Several weeks later, the host told her because she felt she had a right to know. For a few minutes after, it had felt like the world had stopped. When she finally focused again on the conversation, she'd said thank you and then left to go home. Jason hadn't even tried to deny it when she'd asked him. And that was that. The relationship was over.

Chapter Fourteen

Izzy looked at her watch. She still had ten minutes before Trent was due to arrive. In front of her were some of her photo albums. She'd been looking through them since she'd got home from work. The pages were mostly filled with photos of her childhood, and in so many of them, there she was, standing between her parents, all of them smiling. Just the three of them. She picked up one of her favourite photos. She smiled at her twelve-year-old self, standing on the balcony of the beachfront unit her parents had rented on the Gold Coast, the ocean glistening behind her. Izzy had spent most of her time in the water, only getting out when there was a promise of a trip to a theme park or a double scoop of ice cream. Looking at the photo now, she wondered what it would have been like to share that holiday with someone else. Izzy stared at the photo until she heard Trent's car pull up then quickly put it away. She opened the front door to let him in, and she saw Harry standing at the gate.

"I was coming home from my evening walk when Trent pulled up. I was just telling him I had some news for you."

"Do you want to come in for a cuppa?"

"That would be nice. I'm not interrupting your plans, though, am I?

"Not at all. Come in."

Izzy opened the screen door for Harry and then kissed Trent as he followed Harry in. While Trent made a cup of tea for Harry and coffee for them, Harry started talking.

"I was at the bowls club last night. I play twice a week. Gets me out of the house and helps keep me active. Anyway, I was talking to a friend of mine, Alf. I've known him for years. I was telling him about the diaries you found, and he said he went to school with twins who had parents named Frank and Susannah. The twins were a surprise when they arrived in 1940, a long time after their three other children were born."

"Trent, you need to hear this."

He put the cups down on the dining room table and took a seat while Harry repeated what he'd said.

"Is Alf still in contact with either of the twins?" he asked.

Harry shook his head.

"Oh no," Izzy said. "We could have been so close."

"But we are close," Harry said.

Izzy looked at him. "What do you mean?"

"I'll tell you about Frank, and then I'll tell you about the really exciting news."

Trent laughed. "Not sure Izzy can wait that long."

"It will only take a moment to finish. Anyway, I found out why Frank went off to war when he was older. Turns out he was a dentist and joined the Australian Army Dental Corps in 1943. He went off to New Guinea and died there in 1944."

Izzy hadn't thought of dentists going to war before. She wondered how Frank had felt about going, especially when he hadn't been considered fit enough to fight in the First World War. But that hadn't stopped him from being sent as a dentist in 1943. And it didn't stop him from being killed either.

"That would have been sad for his family," Trent said.

Izzy nodded. "Yes, but it was many years ago now. And apparently, there is exciting news."

Trent laughed again. "Told you she couldn't wait."

Harry smiled and continued his story. "So anyway, Alf was saying that even though he lost touch after school, it turns out his wife's bridge club recently had a new member join. One of the twins—Katherine."

Izzy almost dropped her cup. "What! So you do know someone who knows a living relative of Grace?"

Harry nodded. "I do. Small world, isn't it."

"Wait until Teresa hears about this," Trent said.

Izzy smiled. "She'll be excited, maybe even more than you."

Trent shook his head. "I doubt it. I'm invested now, too, just as much as you and Teresa."

Harry smiled at them. "Nice to see you've got something to work on together. I always found that the time Eleanor and I spent on mutual interests were some of the happiest we had together."

"How long were you married?" Trent asked.

"Ellie and I were married for forty-six years. We courted for two years before that."

"When did she pass away?"

"Three years ago. I miss her every day."

Izzy saw a tear in Harry's eye, and she reached over to hold his hand.

"I'll be fine. Don't worry about me. Now, what about Katherine? I thought I'd ask Alf's wife to tell Katherine about what you've found and see whether she'd be happy to meet you."

"That would be fantastic if you could," Izzy said. "I wonder if Katherine ever came to this house. And how much she can tell us about Grace."

"From what you've read so far, they seemed like a close family, so you would assume that she knew her aunt well," Trent said.

"I hope she wants to meet us," Izzy said.

"I'll ask Alf the next time I'm at the bowls club and let you know what happens."

"You should ring Teresa soon," Trent said after Harry had gone. "She'd never forgive you if you held on to this news."

Izzy laughed. "I know. If we get to meet Katherine, she'd want to be there."

"Maybe I should ring her. I still haven't thanked her."

"For what?"

"If it wasn't for Teresa, I wouldn't have met you."

He kissed her, and Izzy thought, not for the first time, how nice it was to be with someone who cared about her and wanted her to be happy. Then he settled into the lounge chair and turned on the TV to watch the news. Although she was interested in what was going on in the world, she was more interested in dentists going to war. It was something she just couldn't picture. So she turned on the computer to do some research and was surprised to see that dentists had been used in the First World War as well, long before Frank left Australian shores.

Special dental units were formed in 1916 and they had embarked with the troops. Izzy reread those few lines, wondering if Martin had any cause to see one of the dentists. She also wondered if he'd been a patient of Grace's brother, but the more she wondered, the more she doubted she'd ever find out about either of those things. Based on what she'd read of Grace's diaries so far, writing about a visit to the dentist wasn't something she would have detailed, so Izzy went back to reading the information she'd found online. Before 1943, dentists were part of the Australian Army Medical Corps, but in April of that year, the Australian Army Dental Corps was formed. Dentists were sent to many of the theatres of war, including New Guinea, providing dental services to soldiers and support personnel.

The more she read, the more Izzy realised how much sense that made. Just because someone was fighting in a war didn't mean they wouldn't get dental issues and a dentist would be much better placed than a doctor to deal with those issues quickly. But would it have occurred to Frank, or any of the other dentists who went, that when they'd started their dental training, one day they'd be going to war? She tried to imagine how he'd felt, but she couldn't. She hoped that Martin had spoken with him, although

     <u>The Diary and the Green Dress</u>

with everything she'd read so far about his reluctance to talk about his own experiences, maybe he didn't. Maybe Frank had gone with no warning at all of what things would be like.

Izzy continued to read and saw that in 1948, the name was changed to the Royal Australian Army Dental Corps. After World War II, dentists also went to Korea and Vietnam and were part of peacekeeping missions in Somalia, Rwanda, Bougainville and East Timor. The more she read, the more interested she became and the more she wanted to know about her grandfather's World War II service and if he'd ever been in Papua New Guinea. She knew that he'd fought in Europe when most of his contemporaries had fought in South East Asia. Still, she was unsure of where and when and if he'd fought closer to home before he went to the northern hemisphere. And then something occurred to her that hadn't crossed her mind before. Considering he'd fought in Europe, he would have fought against the Germans. So how had he felt when his son came home one day with a German girlfriend? It was something she wanted to find out—if her dad was happy to talk about it.

"Have you got any holidays owing?" Trent asked later as they were preparing dinner.

Izzy nodded. "Yes, a few weeks. Why?"

"I thought we could go away for a week or ten days. One of the Pacific Islands or somewhere in South East Asia."

"I've never been to any of the Pacific Islands, so one of those would be good."

She wasn't ready to go back to South East Asia. The last time she'd gone had been with Jason. He'd spent a few of his childhood years in Singapore when his parents worked there with the embassy, and he wanted to go back and see the places where he'd spent time as a child. Izzy remembered how close to him she'd felt because he shared all of these important memories with her. Jason had shown her the house he'd lived in, the school he'd gone to and the creek where he'd played. He'd even shown her the grave of his best friend from that time who'd been hit by a car. Izzy had thought it meant something, but he'd already started cheating on her just before they'd left on holiday, so it turned out not to be as important as she'd thought. She sighed quietly to herself, so Trent couldn't hear. The more she tried to leave all thoughts of Jason in the past, the more they seemed to want to come back.

"I like the idea of going to a tropical paradise with you. I'll check and see what deals I can find."

Trent kissed her again and went back to cooking. In the background, Izzy could hear her phone ring.

"You must have ESP."

Teresa laughed. "Why do you say that? Have you got something to tell me?"

"Yes, I do."

"Trent asked you to marry him!"

Now it was Izzy's turn to laugh. "We've only been together for seven months."

She paused for a moment, counting in her head. It really had been seven months since Teresa's BBQ. The year was going by too quickly.

"It's too soon for anything like that," Izzy said, thinking those words could apply to an engagement and to Claudia's visit.

"I know people who were engaged after three months."

"Well, I'm not the sort of person who would do something like that. Much too soon for me. We did talk about going on a holiday together, though."

"That's exciting. Where to?"

Izzy spent the next few minutes talking about the proposed holiday with Trent and then moved on to the conversation with Harry.

"I can't believe it!"

"I know. It's amazing, isn't it? If we do get to meet Katherine, we'll have to think carefully about all the things we want to ask her in case we only get one chance."

"I wonder if she knows anything about Bryce."

Izzy thought about what Teresa had said after she hung up. She couldn't see how they could ask. If Katherine didn't know, they would be betraying Grace by telling her secret. But if she did know, she could answer the one question they all had. Was Grace ever able to confirm if it was Bryce or Martin who was Hettie's father? She also made a note in her calendar to visit the local historical society the following week and see what information she could find about her house, Grace, her family, and the factory. It might give them more of a picture and help them think of the right questions to ask. She'd been thinking about the historical society ever since Teresa first mentioned it, but she hadn't got around to doing it yet. There had been too many other things going on.

The following week came, though, and Izzy's plans changed suddenly. Trent found a last-minute, half-price holiday deal, so Izzy found herself preparing to go on holiday much sooner than she thought.

How's the packing going? Teresa's text read.

Almost done. Just need to pack my hat and sunscreen.

I'm so jealous. I'd love to be lazing around on a beach in Vanuatu for a week with a cocktail in my hand.

I'll send you a photo.

Gee, thanks. Have a great time. Can't wait to hear all about it.

As they stood in line waiting to check in their bags, Izzy looked around the airport. It was busy, noisy and she could hear a multitude of accents. In only a few months from now, Claudia and her family would be standing in this airport, looking around as she was now, hearing the same noises and the different accents. How much thought had Claudia put into the decision to come before she'd told them? And how much had she thought about the visit since then? Not a day went by when Izzy didn't think about it, even if it was only briefly. She hoped by thinking about it, she would be prepared. However, no matter how many times the visit drifted into her thoughts, she still couldn't picture them getting off the plane and walking through the area she was now standing in. Nor could she imagine what would happen when they stepped out of the airport on the day Claudia would have her first in-person meeting with her father, her family in tow. Her and Izzy's father.

Three hours later, Claudia's visit was still on her mind despite the movie she'd watched and the conversation she'd had with Trent, the plane came in to land. Izzy looked out the window, and the first thing she saw were palm trees, followed by cows in a paddock next to the runway. The only thing keeping them off the tarmac was a thin wire fence. Izzy kept her eyes on them as they landed, but none of them so much as looked up. As she stood in the airport, the smallest one she'd ever been in, she already felt relaxed, like she'd been on holiday for a few days already. On the journey to their hotel, she looked out the window, not wanting to miss anything. And for the first time that day, her thoughts about Claudia's upcoming visit slipped from her mind.

When they got to their room, Izzy opened the balcony doors, looked at the ocean view and felt the breeze coming off the sea. She was determined not to let those thoughts back in for the rest of the holiday. In the distance, she could see two cruise ships anchored, their passengers no doubt exploring the island somewhere, something she and Trent would do the following day. All she wanted to do for the rest of that day was swim in the pool, sip a cocktail with an umbrella in it, and then head to the bar next to the main resort pool and listen to the musician she'd seen advertised on the sign in the reception area. Izzy wasn't even thinking ahead to dinner. It had been a long time since she'd had a holiday and with everything that had been going on, thinking only an hour or two in advance was enough.

After a late night, which included fresh seafood for dinner and a show featuring traditional dancers, singers and fire twirlers, they stood outside the resort the following morning ready to begin exploring.

There were options for day tours from the resort, but Izzy thought hiring a local driver would be more fun. She'd done it in a couple of other countries, although those weren't trips she wanted to think about, mostly because of who she'd travelled with. They hadn't been outside long when a line of taxis pulled up, all the drivers jumping out and running over to

        <u>The Diary and the Green Dress</u>

them, each trying to push the others out of the way.

"Best price. Best price," they called.

Trent turned to look at Izzy. "They can't all be the best price."

Izzy smiled and told him it was how things worked as she walked up to the driver with the car that looked the least likely to fall apart. And then the haggling began. Sometimes Izzy enjoyed it; other times it annoyed her. Luckily that day, she was enjoying it. Before long, she and Trent were in the back of the taxi, a price negotiated for the day that was half the price of the organised trip from the resort.

By the end of the day, they'd seen a beautiful waterfall, visited a village, and met some of the inhabitants. The children were excited to see them, especially when Izzy handed them some lollies from her bag. Then they saw giant turtles and coconut crabs on the beach and swam in crystal clear water. They finished the day at the botanical gardens, perched high on a hill that had a fantastic view of the island and the surrounding ocean. From their vantage point, Izzy could see that more cruise ships had arrived.

All day their driver had been chatting to them, telling them about the island and its history. And more than once, he told them they were one of the most well-suited couples he'd ever met. Even though she'd heard flattering comments from drivers just like him on previous occasions, all in the hope of getting a bigger tip, she'd never heard any of them say that. And she was surprised at how much she liked hearing it.

The rest of the days went by in a blur. They swam, snorkelled, kayaked, walked on the beach, had massages and went to the markets to buy souvenirs for their families and friends. On the last night, they had dinner at a restaurant they'd discovered earlier in the week, wanting to eat coconut crab one more time. As she ate, Izzy found herself wishing that it wasn't their last night. Everything had been peaceful and happy, and she hadn't needed to give too much thought to anything until now.

"What do you think about moving in together?" Trent asked.

Izzy almost choked on her coconut crab and had to take a sip of water.

"I guess you weren't expecting me to say that."

Izzy shook her head.

"I've been thinking about it, though. We spend most of our time together, and it makes sense not to be paying for two households. And I'm not planning on going anywhere."

It wasn't the first time Izzy had heard that from someone, but this time it felt different.

"I suppose it does make sense."

"More importantly, do you want to?"

Izzy asked for a few minutes to think about it, and Trent waited patiently while she did. The more she thought about it, the more she realised it was time to get over her fear and take a chance. He smiled when she nodded, then leaned over and kissed her. Trent ordered champagne, and as they drank it, they discussed the practicalities. By the time the champagne was gone, the decision had been made that Trent would move in with Izzy as her house was bigger and closer to where they both worked. They'd rent out Trent's house, and he'd contribute towards Izzy's mortgage as well as split the household bills. Izzy couldn't believe how easily they agreed on everything, especially the money side of things. When she'd lived with Jason, he argued about every cent he paid towards anything.

A week later, as she walked around her house wondering what it would look like with Trent's things there, she still couldn't believe how easy the discussion had been. She just hoped living together would be easy too. When she got to the bathroom, she stopped for a moment, then turned back to the hall cupboard, took out another towel and hung it beside hers. She was still looking at both towels when she heard a knock. On the other side of the front door was Harry's smiling face.

"Alf's wife has spoken to Katherine. She's in Sydney at the moment visiting one of her grandchildren who has just had a baby. She's very excited about being a great grandmother."

As lovely as being a great grandmother would be, all Izzy wanted to know is whether she'd agreed to meet. When Harry nodded, Katherine wasn't the only one who was excited about something.

"Did they know each other well?"

Harry nodded again. "She and Grace were very close, and she'd love a chance to see the diaries. I'm not sure when she'll be back, though."

Izzy couldn't wipe the smile from her face. It didn't matter when Katherine came back. All that mattered is that she agreed to meet them.

After Harry left, Izzy made two phone calls. Teresa was so excited that she wanted to get on a plane to Sydney the next day. Trent was more subdued in his response, happy to meet Katherine but also happy to wait until she came back. He'd also spent the whole day going from room to room, deciding what he would throw out before the packing began. Izzy had offered to help, but she didn't know what Trent wanted to get rid of and what he didn't, so she said she'd help when the boxes were ready to be filled. It hadn't been that long since the last time Trent moved, and she knew he hated doing it, so it meant even more that he was willing to do it for her. After she'd made the phone calls, she picked up a diary. She didn't know how soon they'd get to meet with Katherine, and she still had a few to go.

4 October 1923

Martin came home today. He didn't say anything in the car on the way back. Instead, he spent the whole journey staring out the window. Thankfully Father drove the car. It would have been too hard to bear if Bryce had been driving. There is no way we can see each other now that Martin is back, and there is no reason for Bryce to come over anymore. After we got home, Martin sat in his chair in the parlour and didn't move until I told him that dinner was ready. He didn't say anything while we ate, and soon after, he went to bed. It was strange sleeping next to him again.

11 October 1923

Martin has been home a week. He does not refer to the time he was away. He hasn't said anything about what it was like at the rest home, his treatment or what the doctors said. I wish he would say something. I feel like I don't know him. And I wish I could see Bryce.

15 October 1923

We went to Mother and Father's for lunch today. Martin didn't say very much at the table and then went into the study afterwards with Father. He thinks the sooner Martin gets back to work, the better and that working will help him fully recover. While Martin and Father were in the study, Bryce came in. He had some papers that Father needed to sign. Mother was there the whole time, so I couldn't say anything except exchange a few pleasantries. I wanted to say so much. I couldn't stop looking at him, and I hope Mother didn't notice. While he was there, it almost felt like my heart was smiling. That is a strange thing to say, but I can't think of any other way of describing it.

16 October 1923

I've been thinking about Bryce ever since I saw him yesterday. And I've been thinking about what it must have been like for him to see Hettie at my parent's house, knowing Martin was there. She had been asleep when he came in but woke up while he was in the study, and Agnes, the new housekeeper, brought her to me. I was holding her when he came out of the study, and he looked right at us.

21 October 1923

Martin came to church today for the first time since he's been back. Father Stewart spoke to us and told Martin he was happy to see him and hoped he was feeling better. The other parishioners stared at us when we walked in and then, after the service, said hello to him like he'd been there last Sunday. Bryce was there too. He was sitting a few rows behind us. Even though I couldn't see him, I knew he was looking at Hettie and me.

23 October 1923

When the doctor released Martin, he said it would be better for his recovery to be at home with his wife and child, but I think it's too soon. He doesn't sleep at night, and during the day, he sits in the parlour and stares at the wall. Mother has noticed, but she keeps reassuring me that he will be fine. He just needs a little more time, and I should focus on looking after him until he's well. But who is focused on looking after me? Even though Hettie brings me so much joy, not a day goes by when I don't think

     <u>The Diary and the Green Dress</u>

of Lily. Or worry that what happened to Lily could happen to Hettie.

5 November 1923

I saw Bryce today. He came to pick up Martin for his first day back at work. I'm not sure he's ready, but I think he feels he has to go as Father keeps telling him that working will be good for him. Martin hasn't fully recovered, though. I still can't tell if he ever will.

12 November 1923

Mother and Father have just been to visit. When Mother said that Hettie looked just like me, I felt a weight lift from my shoulders. Especially as it seems she's going to have wavy hair. Mine is straight, and so is Martin's.

8 December 1923

Tonight, we had a family celebration as Father has decided to retire. He told everyone he's handing over the running of the business to Martin. In reality, it will be Bryce who keeps things running. I saw Bryce at the party. We said hello to each other but not much else. I couldn't risk it. He complimented me on my dress. It was the mint green one Mother and I made for the dance I went to with Frank and Susannah. Several other people commented on it as well. Bryce left early, but he gave me a letter as he was saying goodbye. No one saw him do it. I haven't opened it yet.

Chapter Fifteen

Izzy found herself free Saturday morning, so she decided to stop saying she needed to go and visit the local historical society and actually do it. As she waited to speak to the volunteer, whose name tag said 'Gwen', she was surprised at how many people were there. Five in line in front of her and seven others looking at the items on display. On her way there, she'd assumed she'd be the only one visiting, but from where Izzy was standing, she could see why it was popular. The small space was crowded with items, all telling stories about Brisbane's past in one way or another. On the walls were photos of the city over the years and framed copies of *The Telegraph* and *The Brisbane Courier.* To Izzy's left, there was a cabinet displaying postcards and drawings of Brisbane from the 1870s onwards. Behind Gwen, there was a gramophone with a record on it. And to Izzy's right, glass cases containing dresses and suits, one of the dresses not unlike the one Grace made that she had at home. She slipped out of her place in line and read the card, '*Evening dress, 1922*'.

When her turn finally came, she was delighted by how passionate Gwen was. Not only about the history of the whole city but, more importantly, the history of the inner northern suburbs, including the one where Izzy lived. And once Izzy told her what she was looking for, Gwen said she couldn't wait to get started and see what she could find.

"Almost all of our records are online now. We still have the originals, but we've scanned most of them, so it's easier for people to search. I'll bring up a few records so you can start reading while I keep searching."

The first record Gwen brought up contained photos of the factory owned by Grace's father, and in the first one, he was standing in front of the building. There was no date in the caption, but it must have been taken when he was older because he had grey hair and a grey beard. He stood straight and tall, with an uncomfortable expression on his face. The next photo was the factory again, but there were no people in it. The factory itself was large—a long rectangle shape, made of brick, standing two stories high. In the photo, there was smoke coming out of the smokestacks. The caption said the factory produced building materials, and Izzy wondered if that's where the materials for her house had come from. She moved on to the last photo Gwen had found.

It was similar to the first, but in this one, a man was standing in the doorway just behind Grace's father. She read the caption, and the name grabbed her full attention—Bryce MacDonald. She made the photo bigger so she could see him clearly. Even without knowing much about him, Izzy could see how Grace had fallen for him. He was very good looking—tall and well-built with a smile on his face that conveyed warmth and compassion. As with the photos they'd seen of Grace and Martin, she couldn't tell the colour of Bryce's eyes either because this one too was a black and white photo. And even though his hair was cut short in the style of the day, she could see it was wavy.

"I've found a photo of your house," Gwen said, interrupting her thoughts.

Izzy paused for a moment, torn between looking more closely at Bryce and seeing a photo of her house. But Gwen was waiting for her, so she got up and went over. It was her house, but it had changed over the years since the photo was taken. Back then, there was only a verandah along the front and possibly the back—it was hard to tell from the photo, but Izzy thought she could see part of a railing on the back right corner of the house. At some point after the photo was taken someone had added the side verandah. The stairs in the photo led straight up from the street instead of sideways against the house as they did now, and there were two windows, which were no longer there, on either side of the front door. The road in front was dirt, and there was no fence around the yard.

"I've also found a few references to Grace," Gwen said. "And a photo of her and Martin."

Grace wore a drop-waisted dress, similar in style to the one Izzy had but without the beading, a cloche hat and shoes with a small block heel and rounded toe. Martin, wearing a suit, was standing stiffly beside her. In the background, Izzy could see a church, which made sense when she read the caption '*Church picnic January 1920*'. Izzy looked at the photo and thought about all the things that would happen in the next few years—Lily being born and then dying, Martin going away, the affair with Bryce, and then Hettie's birth. All of that was ahead of them when the photo was taken, and there was no way for them to know what was coming.

"Here's an article from a newspaper that mentions them as well," Gwen said. "There's a photo with it too."

The article, dated 10 December 1923, was about Grace's father retiring. It talked about how he opened the factory in 1879 when he was nineteen and how it had been one small building and two employees. Over time he built it up, bought the land next door, expanded the factory and now there were one hundred and thirty employees. The article quoted Grace's father several times, talking about how proud he was of his achievements and how important the factory had been to him since the beginning. Now, it was time to retire and let someone younger take over the running of the business. There was no mention of who was taking over, although she could see Martin in the accompanying photos. She also saw Grace's mother for the first time, and the resemblance was unmistakable. They were the same height, had the same build, and their facial features were almost identical. The only difference Izzy could see between them was that her mother's overall appearance was more formal, from the dress she was wearing to her grey hair tied back in a bun. If Izzy hadn't known when the photo was taken, she would have assumed it had been taken several years earlier when fashions were different. Izzy turned her attention to Grace. She was in the last photo with Martin and her parents. She looked tired, and the hopefulness that had been on her face in the first photo was no longer there. Instead, it had been replaced by the realisation that life was not always fair. Her hair was much shorter, and from the way Grace was standing, it looked like she was slightly hunched over, as if she was trying to hide, not wanting the camera to capture her as she was then.

"That's all I've been able to find today," Gwen said. "I can keep looking and contact you when I find more."

All the way home, Izzy thought about the photos she'd seen, especially the last one. She couldn't get it out of her mind. Grace looked like she didn't have the energy to make it not only through that day but also the

     <u>The Diary and the Green Dress</u>

ones that would follow, and Izzy wondered if anyone had noticed. And if someone had, did they help Grace in any way? It was silly to think, but Izzy wished she could go back in time and be there for Grace. Tell her that she would be all right and she wouldn't be sad forever. That even though her life had been turned upside down, she was strong enough to get through it. Just as Teresa had done for Izzy when she'd needed it. Even though what Grace experienced was worse than what Izzy had been through, she knew the difference having someone in your corner made.

She was still talking to Grace in her head when she arrived home. However, the one-way conversation ended abruptly when she saw an email from Claudia waiting for her.

Hi Izzy

We are all excited about our upcoming trip to Australia. The children talk of nothing else and can't wait to go to the beach. I've told them the trip is not just about the beach; the most important thing is meeting family. They understand and ask questions about our father and about you. Eventually, though, they start talking about the beach again!

I've booked accommodation in Brisbane and on the Gold Coast. I've also arranged our flights, and we arrive in Brisbane on 20 December and leave on 8 January.

I'd like us all to spend Christmas Day together so I thought it would be good to arrive a few days before to get to know each other. I mentioned that to our father when I spoke to him earlier today.

Izzy looked up from the screen. For the past two years, it had just been Izzy and her parents on Christmas Day, and it had been lovely. They'd started on Christmas Eve, attending Christmas Carols in a local park and then Izzy had spent the night sleeping in her childhood bedroom. In the morning, they'd eaten breakfast together, opened their presents and then begun preparing the food. After lunch, all three of them had fallen asleep, the result of overeating and a few glasses of wine in the middle of a hot summer's day. It had been late afternoon before Izzy went home. This year was her first Christmas with Trent, and they'd already agreed that he would spend the day with her family. Now Claudia, her husband and their children would be there as well. Christmas was her favourite time of year, and she always looked forward to it. So many things had changed for her already, and she wasn't sure she was ready for Christmas to be so drastically different. Should she have tried talking Claudia out of coming at Christmas and instead suggested that she and her family visit at another time of year? Izzy returned to Claudia's email.

He said he would speak to you about it. He also said he would talk to your mother. We haven't spoken very much about your mother in any of our conversations, but I imagine finding out about me was a shock for her as well. I hope she is happy to meet us.

I also spoke to our father about spending some time at the beach with us. Not just him, but your mother and you and Trent as well. I would like that very much.

Claudia

Izzy reread the email before she rang her dad.

"I was going to ring you tonight," he said. "I assume you're ringing about Christmas Day?"

"Christmas Day, spending time at the beach and mum."

"I told your mum about the conversation with Claudia and what her plans were. She said she needs to think about it before we talk some more."

"Was she upset?"

"At first, but now I think she's wavering between her feelings and doing the right thing for Claudia and her family."

"How do you feel about it?"

"I still can't believe Claudia exists. Half the time, I'm not even sure what to say when she rings, let alone what I'll say when we meet. I want to spend time with her and get to know her. So, regardless of what we do at Christmas, I'll go to the beach for a few days. If your mum doesn't want to go, I'm not going to try and talk her into it. If you don't want to go, that's fine as well."

     <u>The Diary and the Green Dress</u>

Izzy thought about their conversation for a long time after they hung up. Her dad wasn't one for dramatic displays of emotion. Even if he was, it wouldn't be necessary this time. She heard everything she needed to in his voice.

A few days later, after speaking with her dad and eventually her mum, she replied to Claudia's email.

Hi Claudia

Thanks for the details about the trip. We're all looking forward to meeting you and your family and are glad you're spending Christmas Day with us. It will be a different experience for you this year; an air conditioner and a pool instead of a fire; prawns, ham, chicken and salads instead of a roast meal; a swim in the afternoon instead of walking through the forest.

Looking forward to spending time with all of you at the beach as well. Don't forget to pack sunscreen and a hat. If you have any questions before you fly out, let me know. See you in December.

Izzy

Izzy closed her computer and hoped she'd done the right thing. What if they didn't get along with Claudia or Andreas, or the children turned out to be unruly, and Christmas Day ended in disaster?

She still had an hour before she had to leave to help Trent pack, so Izzy started on some of her chores, which she'd been putting off. As much as she loved her house, she hated cleaning. She was vacuuming the bedroom when she noticed the diary beside her bed. She looked down at the vacuum and then back at the diary. The floor wasn't that dirty. One more day without a vacuum wouldn't hurt.

9 December 1923

I have read Bryce's letter five times now. I know that he's right about going away, but I wish he wasn't. I, too, have never felt so happy. I know I will never feel that happy with Martin. He's still not the same as before he went away to the war. I'm not sure what the doctors did for those months that Martin was with them.

Even though I feel sorrow about him leaving, I guess I should consider myself lucky to experience such happiness with Bryce, as some people never have that.

14 December 1923

I stared at the dress for a long time before I started to fold it. It is so beautiful and making it gave me joy at a time I needed it. But now, when I look at it, I remember the last night I saw Bryce and my heart breaks. So, I'm putting the dress and Bryce's letter in the timber chest Mother and Father gave me before getting married. If anyone asks, I'll say that someone spilt a drink on it as I left the party, and it's ruined.

5 January 1924

I think about Bryce every day. And when I look at Hettie, I see him too. I don't know if that's my mind playing tricks on me, and I'm seeing something that I want to see but isn't there, or whether I see things precisely as they are.

Izzy looked at her watch, thankful that she didn't have to leave yet because she had to know what Grace wrote next. The first entry in the diary she picked up was from 1939, so she put it down. She picked up the next one, and it started even later. One by one, she picked them up, but she couldn't find one for the rest of the 1920s and most of the 1930s. Izzy searched through them all again but couldn't find the missing years.

Chapter Sixteen

"I looked through them all again but couldn't find any that covered those years," Izzy said as she packed what remained in Trent's hall cupboard into a large box.

"I'm sure you'll find them," Trent said. "You found the last one that was missing."

"But that was easier because we found the entries in a notebook. There is nothing like a notebook or journal or anything else that could substitute for the types of diaries Grace used."

"Maybe they were lost," Trent said. "It's been a long time."

Izzy went back to packing, but she couldn't stop thinking about the years she couldn't read about. Surely those entries had to be somewhere. Grace had been diligent in keeping the diaries, even when she didn't have a lot of time to write in them. It didn't make sense that she skipped so many years and then started again.

Trent stopped emptying the kitchen cupboard and looked over at her "You all right over there?"

Izzy looked down at the set of towels in her hands that she'd taken out of the cupboard over a minute ago but hadn't yet put in the box.

"Yes, I'm fine."

"How about we search your house one more time, just in case?"

Izzy nodded, put the towels in the box and kept cleaning out the cupboard.

For the rest of the afternoon, she put all thoughts of Grace out of her mind as she concentrated on packing. For someone who said he'd had a cleanout, Trent still had a lot of things. And if some of those things accidentally fell off the back of the moving truck on the way, that wouldn't be a bad thing, she thought as she picked up a cream Buddha statue with mirrored tiles around the base and the head; a present from a well-meaning relative that Trent pulled out of the cupboard whenever that person came to visit. It was so hideous that Izzy didn't even want it in one of her cupboards, let alone on display if the relative came to her house. She looked at the statue for a few more seconds before putting it down and leaning against the wall. In the next room, she could hear Trent moving around. There was no turning back now. Things were going to change. Trent's family and friends would come to her house, his belongings would be in every room, and hers would have to move to accommodate them. He'd be there when she did her weekly hair treatment, a face mask popped on at the same time. He'd see the days when she wasn't in the best mood and didn't feel like talking, the days she couldn't be bothered tidying up the house and the days when she wanted to stay in her pyjamas until the afternoon. He'd see all of that. She took a few deep breaths before continuing to pack. He is not Jason, she said to herself—over and over again.

The next night, needing a break after unpacking and cleaning since 7 am, they checked the cupboards and drawers they hadn't opened during the day, but there were no other diaries.

"They've either vanished, or Grace stopped writing for a while," Trent said. "We'll just have to start with the next one you found."

"I guess so. I need a shower before we read anything, though."

"Me too. You go first, and I'll order dinner. I don't have the energy to cook, and I doubt you do either."

As Izzy stepped into the shower, ready to wash away the sweat, the dirt and the dust, the first thing she saw was Trent's shampoo. She turned around as she shut the glass shower door and saw his toothbrush on the vanity, next to hers in the toothbrush holder. Beside the vanity, the towel rail still held the extra towel she'd put there. Izzy closed her eyes as the water ran over her, hoping it would wash away her trepidation as well.

Izzy hadn't realised how hungry she was until the food arrived. But halfway through dinner, she stopped eating, her stomach twisting itself into

     The Diary and the Green Dress

knots. It was only the first day, but Trent already looked at ease living in her house.

"What's wrong?" Trent said.

Izzy shook her head. "Nothing, just tired."

"I am too. But there's something else."

Izzy looked across the table at him, taking a moment before speaking. "I feel a bit nervous about living together."

"Me too. It's a big commitment."

"Really? I never would have guessed. Why didn't you say something?"

"I'm not letting a few nerves get in the way. Anything in life that's worthwhile means taking a chance. And I can't think of anything more worthwhile than being with you every day. Why didn't you say anything?"

Izzy hesitated before giving a brief explanation about what happened with Jason. When she finished, she was surprised at how calmly she'd spoken. And that she hadn't felt any sadness.

Trent reached over and squeezed her hand. "That's not me. And it will never be me. This is a big change for both of us, and we'll work it out together."

Izzy picked up her fork again, the knots slowing untying. Trent was right. Anything worthwhile was worth taking a chance on. It was time to leave the past where it belonged.

"This is the closest in years to the last one we read," Izzy said, sitting down in the lounge room after dinner with Trent and a diary.

16 March 1939

There is a fear that another war is coming. I've heard people say it's unavoidable now. Martin hasn't said anything, and if anyone brings the subject up, he walks away. I have heard him muttering under his breath, saying how could this happen again. Thankfully Martin is old now, al-

though even if he was younger, he still couldn't go. After all these years, there is still something wrong with him.

24 March 1939

Father has been talking about the prospect of another war. He has already spoken to the foreman at the factory about getting prepared to assist in whatever way it can with making materials. Even though he's been retired for a long time now, he can't help himself and still gets involved in what's happening in the factory. For someone who is 79 years old, he is very active. Martin is still in charge but doesn't do any of the day-to-day running. If he wasn't married to me, I'm not sure he'd be there at all. And I know he doesn't have the stomach to get involved in making anything that could one day be used in a war.

25 March 1939

Hettie and I attended the Anzac Day service this morning. Martin didn't come with us. He's never been. He goes to the memorial the day after and stands there and reads the names of the men he knew. I don't think he realises that I know what he does, but I've seen him. I don't ask him about it. He wouldn't tell me. The first time I saw him, I watched from a park across the road, standing behind a tree where he couldn't see me. He stood there for almost thirty minutes, not moving, just staring at the names before putting his hat back on, turning and walking away.

27 March 1939

Matron also thinks there will be another war. She wishes that weren't the case, but she too says that it's inevitable. And that when it happens, there will be a need for doctors and nurses. After being a nurse in the last war and seeing things she can never forget, I can understand why she wouldn't want any of the younger nurses to go through the same thing. But she also said that there will be a need for nurses at the hospital when they go, so if I was still interested, she could start my training. I'm very excited by the prospect, although I wish the reason for this opportunity was different. After Hettie was born, I stopped volunteering at the hospital, but as she grew older, I started again. Training to be a nurse has been in the back of my mind, but I never thought I would get the chance. I know there will be objections. Mother and Father will have something to say, but I

     <u>The Diary and the Green Dress</u>

am too old and set in my ways to pay attention. I always thought, as I got older, they would eventually stop worrying about what I was doing and what people would think. But they haven't, especially Mother. Even at her age, behaving appropriately is still very important. I think after everything that has happened in my life, the time for behaving appropriately has passed. I don't think Martin will care if I start nursing. Most of the time, he doesn't seem to notice I'm there.

2 April 1939

Hettie is such a lovely young woman. She knows her mind and can be very strong-willed. She is at an age where young men are showing an interest in her, but she doesn't seem interested in any of them. We went to the annual church picnic today, and several of the young men spent time talking to her. She was polite to all of them but didn't seem to want any of them to stay. All of them mentioned signing up if a war starts. Each time Martin heard one of them say that, he turned away. Hettie noticed and asked him why, but he didn't answer. She didn't ask again, and she hardly spoke to him for the rest of the day. That's not unusual, though. Martin and Hettie have never been that close. Even when she was little, Martin kept his distance.

Izzy put down the diary and turned to Trent. "I wonder if Martin ever twigged that Hettie might not be his?"

"Maybe. It could be lots of reasons though—Lily, the war."

"It would be interesting to find out more about Martin's war experiences."

Trent nodded. "Maybe there will be something in the remaining diaries. And weren't there letters in the trunk? There could be something in one of those."

"Good idea. I'll go and get them, and we can have a quick scan and see."

But before she got up off the lounge chair, she heard a knock on the door. When she opened it, Harry was standing there.

"Hope you don't mind me coming over so late."

Izzy had to suppress a smile. 7.30 pm wasn't late. "Of course not. Come in."

"I was thinking about the other day when you mentioned a Bryce in the diaries. It occurred to me a few minutes ago that I had met a Bryce. He came here to the house. It was sometime in the 1960s. I can't remember the year exactly. I saw him over the fence, and he waved and introduced himself."

"I wonder if it's the same one."

"I don't know, and I'm not sure how we find out."

"We?"

Harry laughed. "Yes, I'm hooked now too."

Izzy had just invited Harry in and shut the door when she heard another knock.

"Hope you don't mind me stopping by," Teresa said. "I'm just on the way back from visiting my sister, and I thought I'd call in. How's the moving in going?"

"It's going well. Better than I expected."

"I can't wait to hear about it."

"Well, you'll have to wait. Harry is here, and he has more news."

"It has to be the same person," Teresa said when Harry finished telling her and Trent what he'd told Izzy.

"If it is, there would have been many years between the last time Grace and he saw each other and when Harry met him," Trent said. "Maybe it's not the same person."

"It has to be," Teresa said.

Izzy laughed. "You think it was the same person because you want it to be."

"Of course I do. Don't you? And besides, how do we know they didn't see each other between the last mention in the diary and when Harry saw him. Didn't you say there were a lot of years not covered in the diaries?"

"You think they might have met again when Hettie was a child?" Trent said.

"I don't know, but surely if he had any inkling that Hettie was his daughter, he would have tried to see her at some stage."

Harry shook his head. "Things were different back then. Even if he did think Hettie might be his, Bryce wouldn't come back if he thought he would do any harm to the life Grace and Hettie had."

As she had each time she thought about it, Izzy felt sad for Bryce. He would have known the likelihood of Hettie being his was very high, yet he couldn't be part of her life. Did he ever come back from Melbourne and see her when she was growing up? Even if it was from a distance. Had he contacted Grace over the years and asked about her? And if Hettie ever found out about her mother's affair with Bryce, she would have realised she'd grown up with a man who probably wasn't her father. It was hard not to think of the similarities with Claudia, although in her case, she'd known for sure that the man she grew up with wasn't her father. And he knew he wasn't her father either. The only person who hadn't known was Ben, Claudia's actual father. It was all very complicated, and Izzy was grateful that up until recently, her family life had been simple. But now that had changed, and she wondered if it would stay complicated or whether they'd find a way to make things simple again.

"I suppose that makes sense," Teresa said. "It's not what I wanted to hear, though. And I guess without diaries for those missing years, we'll never know. Did you ever see him again?"

"I saw him a few times after that day but not before."

"Maybe after all those years, they were finally together again," Teresa said.

"It's a lovely thought if they were," Izzy said.

"I wonder if he met Hettie," Teresa said, echoing Izzy's thoughts.

"I don't know how well she knew him, but the day he introduced himself, Hettie was there. It was the only time I saw them both here at the house."

"This is getting better," Teresa said. "It's beginning to sound like the makings of a soap opera. We need to organise that meeting with Katherine."

"As soon as she's back, I'll organise it," Izzy said. "Now, how are we going to figure out if it was the same Bryce?"

"Did you see any photos of him at the historical society?" Harry asked.

"Yes, but it was taken a long time before you met him."

"If we can get a copy of that photo, I might be able to tell if it was the same man."

"I'll go and see Gwen and ask if she can find anything."

Saturday morning, Izzy was back at the historical society. In the excitement of getting the photo of Bryce so that Harry could hopefully confirm it was the same person, she forgot about the letters that were in the trunk.

Gwen smiled as she walked in. "Back again so soon."

Izzy nodded and asked for a copy of the photo.

While she waited, Izzy looked around the room. She could spend so much time learning all sorts of things about where she lived and the surrounding areas. She walked over to one of the tables, flicked through a large book filled with information, and started reading about an air raid shelter built in 1942 on Enoggera Road at Newmarket. Izzy peered closely at the accompanying photo and saw that it was now a bus shelter.

"Interesting isn't it," Gwen said when she came back. "There were around 235 air raid shelters built in Brisbane during World War II in case they were ever needed. Some of them still survive, like the one you're reading about."

"So many things in my city that I don't know."

Gwen nodded. "My grandmother lived here during the war and she told me many stories. My favourite is about the American sailor she dated for a while. She was eighteen and he wanted to take their relationship much further, much more quickly, than she was comfortable with."

"It wasn't like he was going to stay either. I imagine he was shipped out somewhere."

Gwen nodded. "He was, although, they wrote to each other until he passed away."

"Really? For all these years? That's amazing."

"Yes, it is. And no matter how many times I tried to get grandma to use email and how many times his grandchildren tried the same thing, they still preferred handwritten letters sent by post. Grandma has a box full of them, including the very first letter. That's why she wouldn't change, she told me once. The first one, and all those that came after, had been hand-written, and she wanted the last one to be exactly the same."

Izzy thought about those letters all the way home, still amazed they'd continued to write to each other. She hoped Gwen would get to read them someday if her Grandmother allowed her to. It would be fascinating to read about their lives over the years, just as it was to read about Grace's life. And in Gwen's case, if she got to read any of them before her grandmother passed away, which given her advanced age could be very soon, she could ask questions and not have to rely on other sources to try and piece together the whole picture. Hopefully, the photo Gwen had copied for her would get them closer to seeing a more complete picture of Grace's life.

Later that day, as she watched Harry look at the photo, she tried not to hurry him along. He'd picked it up and put it down twice now, thinking back to all those years ago. Eventually, he put it down for the third time and left the room for a minute before coming back with a magnifying glass.

"Yes, that's him. Of course, he was a lot older when I met him, but that's him."

Chapter Seventeen

Izzy pulled out the note Harry had given her with Katherine's phone number and the date she was back in Brisbane. If Katherine had come back when she'd planned, she would have been home for three days. That should be enough time for her to settle back in after her trip, Izzy thought, so she picked up her phone and rang the number.

"Hello."

"Hello, is this Katherine?"

"Yes, it is. Who am I speaking to?"

"This is Isabel. Harry, my neighbour, passed on your number to me."

"Oh yes. You're the one who lives in Aunt Grace's house."

Izzy could barely contain her excitement. She was talking to someone related to Grace. Someone who had known her in person and not just through words on a page. Someone who had spent time with her and knew about her life. How much of Grace's life Katherine knew about was yet to be determined, especially where it concerned Bryce. And possibly Hettie.

"Is it still okay if we meet? I'd love to find out more about Grace and your family."

"Yes, I'd like that. I'm intrigued to see Aunt Grace's diaries."

You'll be more than intrigued if you don't know about Bryce, Izzy thought to herself before organising a time the following weekend. Katherine said she would come to Izzy's because she wanted to see the house again. The last time she'd seen it was just before Grace passed away.

After they ended the call, Izzy's thoughts turned to another visit. Before she knew it, Claudia would be here, along with her family. All she knew about them was what she'd read in Claudia's emails. Like with the diaries, reading about someone was very different from meeting them in real life.

By the morning they were going to meet Katherine, Izzy had read almost all of the diaries and had spent a lot of time thinking about what she wanted to ask. She'd talked over some of the questions she was thinking about with Trent, and he added some of his own. He was as excited to meet Katherine as she was. Izzy liked that Trent was involved. Jason had never shown any interest in the things that were important to her. And unlike Jason, living with Trent was easy. And far more enjoyable.

"Coffee's ready," Trent said.

Izzy walked into the kitchen to get her cup. "Let's wait on the verandah so we can see her arrive."

They'd only been outside five minutes before Teresa walked up the front stairs.

"Morning," Trent said. "Didn't think you were going to cancel at the last minute."

"Not a chance. You two look cosy."

"Yes, it's nice out here," Izzy said.

"That's not what I meant, and you know it."

Izzy was about to say something in response when a car pulled up. As Izzy watched Katherine walk up the front stairs, she was immediately struck by the similarities between her and Grace. They both had the same slim build, delicate features and looked to be about the same height if Izzy had judged Grace's height correctly from the photos. She was wearing navy blue pants and a white top with pale blue embroidery around the neckline. Her grey hair was wavy and short. The only jewellery she had on were pearl earrings and a matching ring. She looked much younger than someone who had turned eighty.

"Hello Katherine, I'm Isabel."

"Nice to meet you, Isabel."

"And this is my partner Trent and my friend Teresa."

"Nice to meet both of you as well. I never got to use the word partner in that context. It's not something anyone said when I was your age."

Izzy smiled. "I'm too old to have a boyfriend, so it's the only option I have."

Katherine nodded. "We had boyfriends then husbands. There wasn't anything in between."

"Thank you for coming to meet us," Teresa said.

"My pleasure. I'm happy you found the diaries and want to talk about Aunt Grace. She was my favourite aunt, and I loved her dearly."

"Would you like a tea or coffee?" Trent asked.

"Tea would be lovely."

"Coffee for you, Teresa?"

"Yes, thanks, Trent."

Izzy, Teresa and Katherine made their way to the table on the verandah and sat down while they waited for Trent to come back.

"I was so happy when you rang," Katherine said. "I couldn't believe someone had found Aunt Grace's diaries. I remember watching her write in them when I was a girl."

"Did you spend a lot of time with her?" Izzy asked.

Katherine nodded. "Yes, and a lot of it here in this house. It's strange to be back after all these years."

"Does it look very different?" Izzy asked.

Before Katherine had a chance to answer, Trent returned with the drinks and a plate of biscuits. They waited while Katherine finished a biscuit and had a sip of her tea before starting the conversation again.

"A few things have changed, but not a lot. Grace and Martin did a lot of work to the original house over the years, and Grace continued to make

     <u>The Diary and the Green Dress</u>

updates, here and there, after Martin passed away. She loved this house. She spent a lot of time making it as beautiful as it could be. If anything started to look a bit shabby, she'd spruce it up."

Izzy looked around her. She was glad there was something she and Grace had in common. After the events of two years ago and everything that had happened recently, this house was her sanctuary, and Izzy had every intention of keeping it in the best condition she could. It was also lovely to think she was carrying on Grace's legacy.

"Martin loved the house too. He was more content staying inside the house, though. He didn't spend much time in the garden. I remember Grace saying once he didn't like digging in the dirt."

"What was Martin like?" Izzy asked.

"I had a lot of time for Uncle Martin. He was reserved and didn't say a lot. Some people took that as him being standoffish. He wasn't at all; he was a lovely man. He'd do anything he could for the people he cared about. He just never said a lot or showed any emotion."

Izzy put her cup down and took a deep breath. It hadn't occurred to her before, but she supposed she was an aunt now. Or step-aunt. She didn't know what the correct term was. Would Claudia's children call her Aunt Isabel? Or Aunt Izzy? Or just use her name without the qualifier? Being an aunt was something that had never crossed her mind, having grown up with no siblings. Another thing that had changed in the past few months. And then she had another thought. What would they call their grandfather now that they were soon going to meet him? And hopefully, they were excited that they were going to meet him.

"I never knew Lily, of course, but Grace spoke of her often. So sad."

"Did your parents ever say much about Lily?" Teresa asked.

"Mum mentioned her a few times but not in front of Aunt Grace. She grieved for Lily her whole life, and Mum was cautious not to say anything that would upset her. I don't remember if Dad ever mentioned her. I was so young when he left for the war that I hardly remember him."

"I hope I didn't upset you asking about your parents," Teresa said.

"I forgot how young you would have been when your dad was killed."

Katherine shook her head. "It was a long time ago. It was hard growing up without a dad, but Mum kept his memory alive for us."

"There are a few mentions of your dad and when he passed away in the diaries. Did you want to read them?"

Katherine nodded, so Izzy went and picked up the diary that covered 1944 and handed it to her.

7 February 1944

I can't believe Frank has been killed. He's only been in New Guinea for six months. How does a dentist get killed? I can't imagine he would have been too close to the fighting, but then I don't know exactly what he was doing or where he was stationed. I've tried several times to ask Martin, but he just gives me vague answers and says he doesn't want to talk about it and that it won't bring Frank back by finding out the details. It would make it worse if I knew what happened, he told me. Just remember him how he was. I have some idea of what's been going on, though, from the patients in my care.

Being a nurse fills me with pride, and I love going to the hospital every day to do what I can to help. It gives me a sense of purpose, of being something other than a wife and mother, doing something that is mine, that I have chosen, something that wasn't expected of me. In the back of my mind, I still remember Mother and Father's misgivings when I told them. Neither of them lived to see me complete my training. Father passed away not long after I started, and Mother followed only a few months later. It was like she lost the will to live after her husband died. I consider myself lucky, though. My parents outlived everyone they knew, so I got to spend a few extra years with them, years no one else my age, that I know of, had the chance to do.

The wards are full of men who have come back from the war. Some will talk about what they've seen, and some will try to make it sound like everything is fine and not as bad as what others make out. And some don't say anything at all. They remind me of the men I met at the hospital when I first volunteered all those years ago.

 <u>The Diary and the Green Dress</u>

9 February 1944

I visited Susannah and the children today after my shift at the hospital. I could tell she'd been crying. I can't imagine how hard it will be for her from now on, having five children and no husband. If there is any blessing, it's that the twins, Katherine and Albert, are too young to understand what has happened and what it means. Knowing Susannah, she will do everything she can to make sure the twins know what sort of man Frank was and how much he loved them.

11 February 1944

I've been thinking a lot about Frank. He was such a gentle natured man who never said a bad word about anyone. The only time I ever saw him lose his temper was the fight he had with Father many years ago when he told him he didn't want to work at the factory. Father had always planned that Frank would join the business and then take over from him when he retired. But Frank wasn't the sort of person to run a factory. It wouldn't have suited him. He wanted to help people, not boss them around. They didn't speak for a long time after that, but eventually, they sorted things out. Even though he never said it, I think Father was proud of Frank becoming a dentist.

"Thank you for letting me read that. It's lovely to hear the nice things Grace said about Dad."

"How well did you know Hettie?" Teresa asked.

Izzy shot her a look, but Teresa just shrugged as if to say, we have to ask eventually.

"Very well. She used to babysit my brother and me when we were children. I assume there are mentions of her throughout the diaries."

Izzy nodded.

"Hettie was very different from Grace. More straightforward and confident in who she was and what she wanted."

"There's been no mention of Hettie having a family," Teresa said.

Katherine shook her head. "Hettie never married. She had a lifelong partner. A woman."

"We haven't read anything about Hettie's partner," Trent said.

Katherine shook her head. "Aunt Grace never said anything publicly that I'm aware of, so she wouldn't have written anything down. She just referred to Charlotte, which was her name, as Hettie's best friend."

Izzy, Trent and Teresa looked at each other again. By the expression on their faces, each of them could tell they were all thinking the same thing. Grace may not have written that down, but she wrote something else down she wouldn't have spoken about in public.

"Aunt Grace tried very hard to keep it from Uncle Martin too," Katherine said. "And so did Hettie."

"Would Martin have had trouble accepting his daughter was gay?" Teresa asked.

Katherine nodded. "He might have suspected, but I think he preferred to think that Hettie just wasn't interested in men."

"That must have been sad for Hettie," Izzy said.

Katherine nodded again. "That's how it was then. As far as I'm aware, Hettie and Aunt Grace never spoke to each other about it. There was no one Hettie could talk to. Although I often wondered whether she would have been able to talk to Bryce."

Teresa choked on her coffee, and Izzy put her cup down so quickly that the liquid sloshed over the side of the cup. Trent put his cup down without taking his eyes off Katherine.

"There's a Bryce in the diaries," Trent said.

Katherine sighed. "I shouldn't have said anything. I wasn't thinking. His name just slipped out."

"Did you know him?" Izzy asked.

"Only in later years when he met Aunt Grace again."

"Why shouldn't you have mentioned his name?" Izzy asked.

Katherine paused for a moment before answering. "I don't suppose it matters now. They're both dead, and Bryce doesn't have any children who are still alive, so it won't mean anything to anybody. Except maybe you, depending on what Aunt Grace wrote in the diaries. As far as she was concerned, Bryce was the love of her life. She never stopped loving him, even though they were apart for so many years."

"That must have been awful for her," Teresa said.

Katherine nodded. "At least they got a few years together before Bryce died. Aunt Grace died not long after. Maybe it was a broken heart. She'd certainly had enough heartache in her life."

"Did she ever tell you what caused Lily's death?" Teresa asked. "It wasn't clear in the diaries."

"The doctors said it was rheumatic fever, which was very common back then."

Izzy thought about the woman in the photos and pictured her grieving, sitting by herself crying with no one to comfort her. And she could see her standing by a grave, watching a tiny coffin being lowered into the ground and covered with dirt.

"It wasn't just Lily, though. It was Martin too. Every time Grace spoke about him and what he went through, I would think about my father and what his experience must have been like and how he would have dealt with it if he'd survived."

"Did your mum marry again?" Teresa asked.

Katherine shook her head. "She always said my dad was the love of her life."

Trent reached under the table and held Izzy's hand. She tried not to smile, but it was hard not to.

"At least in the last years of Aunt Grace's life, she had Bryce," Katherine said.

"And Hettie?" Izzy said.

There was silence for a few minutes, and Izzy was beginning to regret mentioning her name. But then Katherine spoke.

"I'm not sure that's something I should be talking about."

"I think we already know," Trent said.

Izzy nodded. "There are a lot of entries in the diaries about the possibility of Hettie being Bryce's daughter, not Martin's."

Katherine was quiet for a moment. "Yes, it's possible. It was never confirmed, but Aunt Grace was sure."

"Did Hettie know?" Teresa asked.

"Aunt Grace told me once that Hettie had asked her. It wasn't long after Bryce came back into her life. Hettie noticed similarities."

"Do you know what Grace told her?" Trent asked.

"She denied it. There was no way to confirm if she was Bryce's daughter, so she didn't see the point in saying anything. It would just cause Hettie pain."

Izzy wondered if Claudia had felt pain. Did she ever wonder how different her life would have been if her mum had stayed in Brisbane? Maybe it was something she could ask at Christmas, depending on how their meeting went. Then Izzy had another thought. If Claudia's mum had stayed here, then she wouldn't exist.

"Are you okay, Izzy?" Trent said.

Izzy nodded. "Just thinking about Claudia and the similarities with Hettie."

"Who's Claudia?" Katherine asked.

Izzy told her about Claudia and what she knew so far.

"Families are complicated," Katherine said. "I can't think of anyone who has a straightforward family."

     <u>The Diary and the Green Dress</u>

Izzy thought that's what she had until she found out about Claudia. Now she wasn't sure what she had.

Chapter Eighteen

"Where shall we sit?" Izzy said, scanning the crowd.

The Remembrance Day service didn't start for another twenty minutes, but almost all the audience seats were filled. Trent spotted two empty seats over on the right in the middle of a row, about halfway down towards the raised stage. There were four seats on the stage and a lectern at the front on the left. As they made their way through the crowd, Izzy was glad to see a lot of children attending with their families. With no First World War veterans remaining and only a few still alive from the Second World War, Izzy thought it was important that their stories were passed on so they wouldn't be forgotten. After politely saying excuse me to several people as they squeezed along the tightly packed rows, they sat down and waited for the service to begin. Izzy watched as a middle-aged man wearing an army full dress uniform led three others on stage. The man directly behind him seemed so frail that Izzy wondered if he was going to make it to his seat without collapsing. When he finally sat down, she breathed a sigh of relief. From the noises around her, she could tell she wasn't the only one thinking that. After the other two were seated, the army captain walked over to the lectern and gave an introduction, welcoming people and going through the order of events. He then moved onto why the ceremony always took place on the same day each year, the day that the guns finally fell silent at the end of the First World War, 11 November 1918. The next person to speak was a woman in her late sixties who had been a nurse in Vietnam. She read two poems, one of them being *In Flanders Field* by John McCrae, which Izzy remembered from a high school history class. Listening to it now, she remembered how the sadness of the words had struck her all those years ago, something they did again that day. The poems were followed by a hymn and a prayer, led by a priest Izzy recognised from a relative's funeral a few years ago. There was a brief pause as the elderly man stood and shuffled from his seat to the lectern. He introduced himself as the last remaining World War II veteran in the area. As he spoke, Izzy sat still, not wanting to miss any of his words; words which spoke of his experiences and of his mates who never came home, some of whom lay in unmarked graves in Papua New Guinea and Thailand. The more he spoke, the more Izzy realised she'd made the right decision to not continue reading the letter she'd found the day before, a letter Martin had written to Grace. It had been stuck inside the back cover of the only diary Izzy hadn't finished. If she hadn't flicked through to see how many pages she had left, she wouldn't have seen it until she'd read the last entries. As she'd held the thin paper in her hands, she'd started reading and then stopped after a few sentences, deciding to wait until after the Remembrance Day service. Izzy knew a veteran would be speaking and thought if she heard about his experiences, it might help her understand a little more about what Martin had written.

After the service ended, following the minute's silence at 11 am and a bugler playing the Last Post, Izzy and Trent walked over to the cenotaph and read all the names. There were so many from both World Wars plus the conflicts since, and they stood and read each one of them. Across from the cenotaph was a concrete wall, the front of which was almost entirely covered by a plaque. On the plaque were the names of the soldiers from the area who'd survived the wars, along with the year they were born and the year they died. What surprised Izzy was not the long list of names but the ages. Some lived to old age, but there were many who'd died between ten and thirty years after they'd come home. Even those who had died thirty years after were only in their fifties, which to Izzy seemed too young to die. Near the top of the list was the name they were looking for – Martin Barclay (1894-1954).

"I see you found his name."

Izzy turned to see Teresa standing behind them. 'I thought you couldn't make it."

"Rob had a last-minute change of plans, so he was able to stay home with the kids."

"If we'd known, we could have tried to get three seats together," Trent said.

"That's all right. I was late, and all the seats were already taken, so

I stood up the back. Is Frank's name here somewhere?"

Izzy nodded and took her over to the cenotaph.

"It's sad to see his name there now that we've met Katherine," Teresa said.

Izzy nodded. It was sad that someone as lovely as Katherine had grown up without a father. But she would have been one of many back then. Just as there would have been many who would have had to call someone else 'father' when their own wasn't there, and they became part of a new family.

"While we're here, we should check another name," Teresa said. "MacDonald."

There was no one with that last name on the cenotaph, so they went back to the plaque. Near the top of the surnames that started with M, there was an Alexander MacDonald.

"By the date of birth, I assume he fought in the First World War," Trent said. "We know Bryce had a big family, so Alexander could be a relation."

Izzy mentally flipped through the pages of the diaries. She couldn't remember any mentions of an Alexander MacDonald, but for some reason, as soon as she saw the name, she was sure they were related.

"I wonder if Katherine knows anything about Bryce's relatives," Teresa said as if she'd read Izzy's mind. "Why don't we get a coffee and give her a call."

Izzy laughed. "Nothing is going to dampen your enthusiasm for this, is it?"

Izzy called Katherine's number. It turned out Katherine wasn't far away and was happy to join them for coffee rather than just talk on the phone.

"I hope we didn't interrupt your plans for the day," Izzy said when Katherine arrived.

Katherine shook her head. "I was just dropping a friend back to an aged care facility nearby. We always go to the service together."

"That's lovely that you both still go after all these years," Teresa said.

Katherine smiled. "She's ninety-seven years old now and lost her first husband during the war. He'd been injured and was coming home, but the ship he was on was sunk by a Japanese submarine."

That's seems so unfair, Izzy thought to herself. He would have been thinking that it wouldn't be long now before he was back with his wife, no longer in a foreign country with a gun in his hand. But the war hadn't been ready to give him back. How many others had that happened to? Almost home, almost safe. But never arriving.

"Did she marry again?" Teresa asked.

"She was still young, so after a few years passed, she met a wonderful man and married him. She still misses her first husband, though. She no longer has her licence, but I've still got mine, so it's the least I can do to take her each year."

"It must have been hard for her with him overseas, knowing the danger he was in," Izzy said.

"It was, but she continued on, just like everyone did back then."

Izzy tried to imagine what it would be like if Trent was fighting in a war, and she was the one waiting at home, hoping he would come home safely, but she couldn't. There was nothing in her life that was even close to something like that. Even the times she'd wondered where Jason was and what he was doing was miles away from worrying whether someone was dead or alive. Although now she realised that even though she'd had no proof until the end, something in the back of her mind had been telling her on more than one occasion that Jason was probably somewhere he shouldn't be.

"Now, what did you want to ask me, Izzy?" Katherine said.

"Do you know if Bryce had a relation named Alexander?"

Katherine paused for a minute. "I'm not sure. There's something familiar about that name, though. What makes you think they might be related?"

Izzy told her about the name on the plaque and the dates next to it.

"It's possible," Katherine said. "It's a common last name, though, so he could have been no relation at all."

"We know," Teresa said. "We just thought it would be interesting to find out."

Katherine nodded. "Let me make a few phone calls. There are still some people I know who knew the family."

In the meantime, Izzy was interested to know about Martin's war service, so when they got home, she went online and looked up his records. He'd served with the 9th Battalion, one of the first infantry units raised by the Australian Imperial Force and the first battalion recruited in Queensland. He'd done his training at Enoggera and then left on the Orient liner Omrah in 1914, heading to Egypt. From there, the battalion headed to Gallipoli, where they stayed until the evacuation in December 1915. After everything he must have seen and experienced there, Izzy wondered what was going on in his mind when he then headed off with the battalion to France. Was he hardened by the things he'd already done or resigned to the fact that he would be there until the end, whichever way that came for him? Martin spent the rest of the war fighting with the battalion in places like Pozieres in the Somme valley and Ypres, in Flanders before participating in the allied offensive of 1918 near Amiens. Izzy didn't know much World War I history but just reading those few lines about the battalion he served in and the places he'd fought went a long way to explaining what she knew of him so far. As she read the information again, she wondered how he would have felt when the Armistice occurred. Was it relief? Or was it relief tinged with the knowledge that he would never again be the person he was before the war? And all those nights, in the mud in the trenches, did he think of Grace? Izzy hoped that he had and that it brought him some comfort.

"I found out that Alexander was related to Bryce, but I don't know how," Katherine said when she rang back after a few days. "I was told that he was the black sheep of the family, though. He wanted to be an artist, which was scandalous for a 'proper' family back then, and moved to Paris to follow his dream."

A family member in Europe, Izzy thought after she hung up the phone. Something she had in common with Bryce.

"Have you heard any more from Claudia?" Izzy asked as she sat down at her parent's dining room table.

Her dad nodded. "Today. The last of her plans, for the visit at Christmas, are confirmed."

Izzy looked at her mum, but she got up from the table, saying she would get the rest of the gravy. Time for a change of subject, Izzy thought to herself.

"Did you get the box out? The one I was asking about."

The Remembrance Day service reminded Izzy of her earlier thoughts about finding out as much as she could about her grandfather's war service. There had been a box in the hall cupboard for as long as she could remember, which was filled with things from when her grandfather was in the army.

Her dad nodded again. "We can look after dinner if you like."

The rest of the meal was spent talking about the changes Izzy was doing at her house, like the new curtains she and Trent had put up the previous weekend. No one mentioned Claudia again.

After dinner, Izzy went through the items in the box—four medals belonging to her great-grandfather along with a faded photo of him in his uniform, the easily recognisable Australian Army slouch hat on his head. In the photo, he looked older than sixteen, although considering he was trying to look older to be able to enlist, maybe that wasn't surprising. She looked closely at the photo again, wondering if the recruitment officer had known he was underage but let him sign up anyway. She also found a note she hadn't seen before, listing all the places he'd fought and the unit he was with. Izzy was surprised to see that even though her great-grandfather had been in a different unit, he'd sailed on the same ship as Martin and had fought in many of the same places. Was it possible they'd met? The more Izzy thought about it, the more she doubted it. So many soldiers had gone to fight that the likelihood of them knowing one another was very slim. They may have briefly crossed paths but even that she doubted.

There were another four medals belonging to her grandfather along with his ration book, pay book, the insignia from his uniform and two photos, each of her grandfather standing tall in his khaki jacket and pants. He looked so young. It had only been her grandfather on her dad's side that fought. Her mum's father had been too young to enlist, not that it had stopped his own father. As she looked at the photos, she wondered if her grandfather had any idea what he had signed up for? Or had he felt that it was his duty, like Martin and Frank?

"Did Grandad know about Claudia's mum?"

Her dad nodded. "He wasn't happy about it at first. After what he'd gone through, the Germans weren't his favourite people. The only Germans he ever spoke to were the guards in the prisoner of war camp where he was kept. When he was fighting, he was focused on staying alive, not speaking with them."

"I didn't know Grandad was in a prisoner of war camp."

"He never spoke about it. I only know because mum told me. I tried asking him once, but he stopped that conversation before I'd even finished asking the question."

"How did he end up there, though? I thought most Australian's fought in the Pacific."

"Mum told me he was an engineer, and some of the engineering units were sent to England and then to Europe. He was captured in 1943 and wasn't repatriated until after Germany surrendered."

"No wonder he wasn't happy about Claudia's mum."

"Eventually, he got used to the idea. It took several meetings before he would even speak to her. But once he did, he came around."

When Izzy went home that night, she couldn't stop thinking about her grandfather, about Martin and Frank and about all the other names she'd seen on the plaque. She fell asleep with her mind still in the past.

    The Diary and the Green Dress

Izzy went back to the past when Katherine came over two weeks later with a letter.

"It was written to my mother by one of her cousins a long time ago now," Katherine said as she handed it to Izzy. "It's not much, but it's something."

The letter contained a sentence that mentioned the cousin having tea with two people she knew when she was younger before they moved to Europe—Alexander and Margaret.

"They were common first names at the time," Katherine said. "But I think it was them."

"I wonder if the historical society could help again," Izzy said. "I'll go back and see what I can find out. Now, let me get the letter I told you about."

Dear Grace

I do not know if I will ever give you these pages to read. Maybe I will tear them up instead. I know you have asked me many times about my experiences during the war, and I have never answered you. If I decide to give this to you, maybe it will provide you with some of the answers you have been looking for.

The first thing I should say is that we had no idea. A great adventure, we were told—an experience of a lifetime. We'd get over there and smash them in a few months and be home for Christmas. It wasn't like that at all. Death and destruction wherever you looked. And mud. The mud was everywhere. I've never been so cold and wet. And the things I saw that were never spoken about.

I wasn't expecting the noise. It would be dark, so dark that you could barely see your hand in front of your face. Then there would be a bright flash of light and then the noise. So much noise that you couldn't think of anything else except wanting it to stop. And then there would be quiet. And then the whistle. Even though we would never admit it, look-ing along the trench, you could see that everyone was shaking with fear but doing their best to hide it. Sometimes I felt like I was frozen in place, and I couldn't go over the top. During those times, someone would grab me and take me over with them. Other times, I was the one who had to grab someone and pull them over. Those were the worst times because often, the mate I pulled over with me didn't come back but lay there in no man's land until someone could go out and get him. Even worse were the times they lay there screaming in pain for hours until they eventually became silent. I remember the faces of every one of those men, and I can't help thinking about what their families felt when they heard the news. I wish I could visit all of those families and tell them I'm sorry, that I wish I had left them in the trenches. But I couldn't do that. I would have been court-martialled, and being thrown in jail was the best possible outcome. The other outcome was the same outcome I lived with every day while I was there. Besides, I couldn't let the others down. They went over, and so did I. Everyone had to do their part, no matter how much they were shaking with fear, so I took them with me.

I can't believe we thought it was going to be an adventure. How stupid were we?

I often see some of the men who live in the area that were in France. We still say hello and talk about the things that are going on in our lives. But no one ever talks about what happened over there. You can tell there are times when someone wants to say something, but none of us does. It would be admitting that we can't handle what we went through, that we're not as brave as we make out we are. No one wants to admit that.

I was scared when you told me you were pregnant. I knew you would say it at some point. We were married, after all. But I wasn't ready when you told me. I didn't know if I could be responsible for another human being. Not after what I'd seen and all those I couldn't help, couldn't protect. But I kept telling myself we'd be safe here. Once I saw Lily for the first time, I fell in love. It didn't stop me from being scared, but she was so perfect. I blame myself for her death. I keep thinking, what could I have done differently? Should I have noticed earlier that she wasn't well? Should I have insisted that we take her to the doctor earlier than we did? Maybe it wouldn't have made any difference, but I can't help thinking I should have done more. Just as I couldn't save my mates in France, I couldn't save Lily.

     <u>The Diary and the Green Dress</u>

"The fear is the same," Katherine said as she gave the letter back to Izzy. "I've read Dad's letters, and he talked about being afraid and not wanting to admit it. Of seeing people die all around him and not being able to do anything. And how much he missed Mum. It meant so much when she received his letters seven months after he died. A friend he served with in New Guinea found them and brought them home to Mum."

Izzy thought about Frank after Katherine left. If he'd survived, would he have been just like Martin?

"Back again," Gwen said as Izzy and Trent walked into the historical society the following Saturday.

"Yes, back for more information," Izzy said before introducing Trent.

"Nice to meet you. What can I help you with today?"

Izzy explained about the plaque they'd seen with Alexander's name on it and asked if Gwen could find more information about him.

"His wife's name is Margaret," Trent said. "If you find any information about a Margaret MacDonald, either the one who was married to Alexander or any others, could you also let us know?"

"Trent thinks the name is familiar, but he can't pick why."

Gwen smiled. "I'll see what I can find out and let you know."

Gwen rang a few days later, so Izzy and Trent found themselves at the historical society for the second Saturday afternoon in a row.

"It's a fascinating story," Gwen said after Izzy and Trent sat down. "As you mentioned to me, he was definitely the black sheep of the family. After World War I, Alexander came back to Brisbane for a while. That's when he married Margaret. But after eight months, they packed up and moved to Paris where he started his art career."

"How was he related to Bryce?" Trent said.

"Oh. I probably should have said that first. It's such an interesting story that I just jumped right in. They were brothers."

Izzy and Trent looked at each other.

"Was he the older or younger brother?" Trent asked.

"Older," Gwen said.

"How did you find out about him?" Izzy asked.

"Alexander MacDonald wasn't as famous as a lot of other artists of the time, but he was well known in the art world, and a lot has been written about him. Including his life here before he went to Paris."

"I didn't even think about looking him up online to see if there was anything," Izzy said.

Trent shook his head. "Me either. What about Margaret?"

Gwen picked up one of the pieces of paper she had. "I couldn't find out as much about her. She was also from Brisbane. Her family had money, and they weren't too thrilled that she married Alexander and went off to Paris. Her family name was Carter."

Gwen passed them one of the photos she'd found. It was a copy of one that had also appeared in an art book that came out in the late 1920s. Alexander looked exactly like Bryce—tall, wavy hair, broad shoulders. He was wearing a white button-up shirt with the sleeves rolled up, black trousers with black suspenders going from the waist up over his shoulders and a pair of black and white Oxfords. What Izzy noticed the most was that he had the same look on his face she'd seen in the photo of Bryce, the one that somehow let her know that he'd been a nice man, someone trustworthy. He was standing at an easel, paintbrush in hand, halfway through a portrait of Margaret, who was sitting on a chair in front of him. She was beautiful, with her dark hair cut into a bob surrounding her oval face. She was staring straight at the camera as if daring it to take her picture. The robe she was wearing was tied around her slim waist but loose enough that it fell slightly at the top, exposing both her smooth and pale shoulders. She was barefoot and wore no jewellery, nor had anything in her hair. She had an air about her that said she knew exactly who she was and what she wanted from life.

"Carter was my great-grandmother's maiden name," Trent said.

"There were a lot of Carters in Brisbane at the time, so it's not surprising that Margaret and your great-grandmother had the same last name," Gwen said.

Later that day, Izzy and Trent scanned the last diary for any mention of Alexander and Margaret but couldn't find any. However, they did find an entry that explained the missing years.

13 March 1968

It's been fourteen years since Martin died. I do miss him. I know we had our ups and downs, but I guess most people do. I've been flicking through my diaries, reading some of the entries about Martin and me. I regret that I stopped writing in a diary for many years. It was too hard at the time with Bryce leaving, Martin not being well, and Hettie growing so fast. I was also guilty about what happened. I learned to let go of that eventually. I couldn't change anything that happened. And after Martin died, I stopped as well. I wasn't sure there was a point in continuing to record all the grief in my life. It's only recently that I've started writing again.

20 March 1968

I've been thinking a lot about Martin and Bryce these past few days. I never wanted to hurt Martin, but I wish I had taken the chance on love instead of doing what I was supposed to.

Chapter Nineteen

Izzy had been staring at the calendar for the past five minutes. No matter how much she stared at it, the date wasn't changing. Arrival day. A few hours from now, Claudia and her family would touch down in Brisbane, and Izzy would be waiting in the terminal to meet them. To keep her mind occupied, she'd organised to meet Teresa for lunch while Trent went back to the historical society. Gwen had called the day before and said she had some information for him. Izzy had heard him talking to her on the phone, but she wasn't close enough to pick up the conversation. When she'd asked him about it later, he hadn't wanted to say anything. Not until he was sure, he'd said, but there was excitement in his voice as he said it. As he'd left that morning, Trent promised he would only be an hour, and then he would head to the café where she was meeting Teresa.

"Are you ready?" Teresa asked once they'd ordered coffees and lunch.

Izzy shook her head. "I thought I'd had enough time to get used to the idea, but now the day is here. I'm a bundle of nerves."

"Maybe caffeine isn't the best idea then."

Izzy shot her a look.

"Just kidding. I expected you to be nervous. Think about what you're about to do."

"I have been. Almost every minute of the past week."

It might sound like an exaggeration, Izzy thought, but it wasn't that far off. She'd done her best to hide it, but she'd been distracted at work, to the point where some of her colleagues asked her if everything was all right; her parents had rung six times to check if she was still happy to pick up Claudia and her family from the airport, and Trent had taken her out three nights during the week to try and take her mind off the day that had finally arrived.

"Have you thought about what you're going to say when you first meet?"

Izzy shook her head. "I've had so many ideas about what to say but no sooner have I thought about what the right thing might be, I change my mind."

As she sipped her coffee, Izzy looked around at the other people in the café. She could see plenty of friends and couples, but she could also see several families. What was their relationship to each other, she wondered? Were they a traditional mum, dad and two kids? Or were they mum, two kids and a new dad? Or a mum with one child married to a dad with another? She tried to picture what the table would look like at Christmas lunch, but she couldn't. Before worrying about Christmas, though, there was still dinner that night to get through, and Izzy hoped for all their sakes that it wouldn't be awkward or end in tears.

"You're not going to believe this," Trent said as he rushed into the café, interrupting Izzy's thoughts.

Teresa put down her coffee cup. "Sounds intriguing. Do you know what we're not going to believe, Izzy?"

Izzy shook her head. "He wouldn't give me any clues."

"Do you remember how I said my great-grandmother's maiden name was Carter?"

Izzy and Teresa both nodded.

"It turns out she had a sister named Margaret."

Teresa turned to look at him. "If you say next what I think you're going to say, I'm glad I'm sitting down."

Trent nodded. "It's the same one."

Izzy put down her coffee cup. "You're not joking, are you?"

Trent shook his head.

"I can't believe it," Izzy said.

"I can," Teresa said. "This is so exciting. And it's another reason the two of you were destined to meet. How did you find out?"

"I remembered that years ago, my aunt put together a family tree. I asked mum to find it for me, and when she did, there was Margaret's name."

Trent opened the bag he was carrying and pulled out a copy of the family tree. On the right-hand side, they saw Margaret's and Alexander's names, along with their dates of birth, marriage and death.

"Margaret and Alexander got married on 19 June 1920," Izzy said. "So not that long after Grace and Martin. I wonder if they were at Margaret and Alexander's wedding. Or if Margaret and Alexander were at Grace and Martin's wedding."

"I don't know," Trent said. "But as soon as I saw the family tree, I called Gwen to see if she could find out anything."

"So that's what the secret was," Izzy said.

Trent nodded. "I didn't want to say anything in case it was just a coincidence with the names, not until I was sure."

Teresa rummaged through the photos and information Gwen had given to Trent that morning. "Here's a photo of a wedding."

Izzy and Trent looked at the photo she was holding. The pose in the photo was almost identical to that of Grace and Martin, with Margaret sitting on a chair and Alexander standing behind her. Their clothes were the same style as well, with Margaret also in a white, floor-length dress with capped sleeves and Alexander in a dark coloured suit. There was something different about this photo compared to the one of Grace and Martin, and it took Izzy a moment to figure out what it was. It was the looks on their faces. Even though, as with Grace and Martin's photo, Margaret and Alexander weren't smiling either, she could tell they were happy, at ease with each other. There was no hint of doubt about the decision they'd made.

Teresa turned over the photo, and on the back, it just said M&A.

"Let's see if there's anything about Margaret and Alexander in the information from Gwen."

Teresa and Trent didn't find anything, but Izzy did—a mention of a party in the 1920s to celebrate Grace's parents' 25th wedding anniversary. Further down the page was the guest list. Some of the ink was faded, but they could make out Grace and Martin's names as well as Margaret and Alexander's. Bryce's name was there too.

"So they did know each other, at least well enough to all be invited to the party," Teresa said.

"No mention of Bryce and Alexander's parents, though," Izzy said.

Trent picked up another piece of paper. "Didn't they own a farm? Maybe it was too far to travel."

They continued to go through the papers Gwen found, most of which covered their lives after moving to Paris. The information focused on Alexander as an artist and Margaret as his muse. Unfortunately, there was very little written about their personal lives. Other than what they'd already found, there was no further mention of them before they left.

Izzy looked up from the pages she was reading. "I wish Grace had continued to write in a diary over the missing years. We could have found out so much more."

Trent nodded. "I wish she had too, especially about the party. I'd like to have read about my relative."

Teresa picked up the photo of Margaret and Alexander. "At least you know what she looks like. I don't have any photos of that generation of my family. No family tree either, although after everything we've been finding out since we read the first diary, I think I might start one."

Trent picked up the copy of his family tree and looked at all the names on it. "I'm going to continue with this one to see how far back I can go. I don't know how easy it will be. As far as I know, no one in the family has any personal papers or letters from back then that might give a clue as to the generations that came before the first one shown here."

"Something else lost to time," Izzy said. "Just like the last diary that ended so abruptly. When I got to the end, I could have sworn there were missing pages."

There hadn't been many pages to go, and Izzy had put off reading them until early that morning because she knew as soon as she did, there would be nothing more to read, nothing more to find out. After all the pages, some with short entries, some with longer, some happy, some sad, some with just entries about day to day life, Izzy felt like she knew Grace. When she closed the back cover, it felt like someone was leaving her life. Leaving on the same day, someone else was entering it. And bringing a husband and three children with her.

"Are you sure it looked like pages were missing?" Teresa said. "Grace could have just stopped writing again."

Izzy shook her head, "It definitely looked like pages had been torn out."

"If they were, I don't think we're going to find them," Trent said. "We searched everywhere when we thought there were other diaries and found nothing."

Trent was right. They'd gone through every cupboard and drawer that had been in the house before Izzy moved in. The only other thing that had been in the house was the trunk. And then she remembered the other envelope, still sitting inside.

It was the quickest trip Izzy had ever taken from the café to home, even though they had to stop at two red lights, each one making Izzy curse, and fifteen minutes later, they were opening the trunk. She pulled out the envelope and emptied the contents.

"More letters from Martin. I can't believe I forgot about this envelope."

Teresa peered over her shoulder. "Anything else?"

Izzy searched through the pieces of paper and shook her head.

"Is that everything from the envelope?" Trent said. "It looks like there's something still there."

Izzy peered inside and saw another envelope, a smaller one that was stuck at the bottom. She pulled it out, opened it and took out the contents.

14 May 1968

Hettie invited me to a fundraiser for the local community centre. She volunteers there in her spare time. Hettie has always volunteered at various places over the years. She reminds me of my mother in that way. I don't want to go, but Hettie keeps saying I need to get out of the house more. Maybe when she's my age, she'll understand that it takes a lot of effort to go out, much more than it used to. Or perhaps the years and the emotions they contain won't wear her down as they have me. She said all I have to do tonight is hand out a lucky door prize ticket to each person as they walk in, and I can sit down while I do it. That sounds easy enough. When I went to the wardrobe to get something to wear, I saw the green dress I made all those years ago. I used to keep it in the timber chest that my parents gave me when I married Martin, but I took it out and put it in the wardrobe a few years ago so I could look at it occasionally. It is such a beautiful dress, and there are so many memories attached to it. But tonight, it made me sad, so sad that I cried, so I put it back in the timber chest. Maybe I should put my diaries there as well. The contents also belong in the past.

"I wonder why she pulled the pages out of the diary?" Trent said.

"Maybe she was going to destroy them at some stage," Teresa said. "What's the next entry say?"

15 May 1968

It took me a long time to fall asleep last night. And for a reason, I always hoped for but never dreamed it would happen. I saw Bryce. I was sitting near the door of the community centre handing out tickets when I heard his voice. "Hello, Grace." I knew it was his voice, even after all these years. I smiled when I looked at him. I couldn't help it. And he was smiling too. Neither of us said anything for a moment. We just kept smiling at each other. And then he said, "it's good to see you," and I knew he meant it. I meant it too when I said the same to him. It's been almost 50 years, but looking at him, those years fell away. He saved a seat for me at the back of the room, away from where all the activities were taking place. When I finished with the tickets, I sat on that seat and didn't move for the rest of the night. I don't think I've ever talked that much. We talked about so many things. He asked about Martin, and I told him we had stayed married until Martin had passed away. I asked if he had married, and he said he had, that they had been married for almost 40 years and that they had been unable to have children. And then he asked about Hettie. I told him how she had grown up, how well she'd done at school and university and where she worked. I didn't mention Charlotte. I also didn't tell him the most important thing - that she was there. I wasn't ready to say it, and I wasn't sure if he was ready to hear it. Thankfully she was so busy with what she was doing that she didn't come over and talk to me while Bryce was there. I don't think she even saw us sitting next to each other. On the way home in the car, I kept the conversation to the fundraiser and how successful it had been. Hettie thanked me for handing out the tickets. If she hadn't asked me to do that, there might never have been another occasion where Bryce and I were in the same place at the same time. And I would still be wondering, as I have all these years, if he was still alive and, if so, where he was. And if I would see him again before my life came to an end.

"Imagine what it would feel like to see someone you loved after almost fifty years," Izzy said.

"I wonder if her feelings for Bryce ever changed over the years?" Trent said.

Teresa shook her head. "I doubt it. I don't think his feelings would have changed either."

"I want to keep reading, but you'll have to leave in a minute Izzy," Trent said.

Izzy looked at her watch. The day had gone too quickly, and it was already late afternoon. She wished she hadn't offered to pick up Claudia and her family. It would have been so much easier to meet when they were all together. As it was, it would be Claudia, her husband and three children—and Izzy by herself. She wouldn't even have Trent with her because she only had a six-seat SUV, and one of those seats was in the back with

     <u>The Diary and the Green Dress</u>

the rest of the boot space.

After making Trent and Teresa promise not to read any more pages without her, she left. There wasn't a lot of traffic on the road, and Izzy was at the airport sooner than she'd expected. As she sat in the car park, she realised she still had no idea what she would say. When they walked out through customs, everything would change. Even though she'd spoken to Claudia several times and had seen photos, sometimes it still didn't seem real. But when Claudia and her family were standing in front of her, nothing would be more real than that.

Chapter Twenty

The time passed quickly, much quicker than Izzy was ready for, and the next thing she knew, Claudia and her family were coming down the escalator. Izzy got up from where she'd been sitting and slowly walked towards her, taking a few deep breaths as she did. There were more similarities between them than she'd initially thought, so many that Izzy felt like she needed to sit down again. The photos only told half a story.

"It's nice to finally meet you, Izzy. Or should I call you Isabel in person?"

"It's nice to finally meet you too, Claudia. And yes, call me Izzy. Everyone does."

Claudia smiled. "Izzy, I'd like to introduce my family. This is my husband Andreas and our children, Heidi, Annamarie and Rainer."

Izzy shook hands with Andreas and said hello to the children. They were a beautiful looking family, and the way the children spoke to her was very polite. She could tell they wanted to ask her lots of questions, but something was stopping them. Maybe Claudia had told them to wait.

"You must be tired after your flight. My car isn't far away. Let's get your suitcases and head off so you can check into your hotel and freshen up before we go to dinner."

Izzy couldn't remember whose idea it had been to all have dinner together on the first night they'd arrived. She assumed it was Claudia who suggested it. She'd waited a long time to meet her father, and she probably didn't want to wait any longer. Izzy would have been happy to wait a little longer. She'd been trying to convince herself that it would be okay to share her dad with someone else ever since she first learned about Claudia, but she hadn't quite managed to do so. She was a lot closer than she had been, though, so that was something. At least they would all be there—Trent, her mum, Claudia's family. A buffer in case things didn't go well. And her dad, their dad. But even though it had only been a few minutes since they'd met in person, Izzy had a feeling that things would be ok.

They waited at the baggage carousel, the focus on looking for their suitcases enough to distract them from trying to make small talk. When all their luggage was collected, they headed towards Izzy's car.

"It's so hot," Annamarie said, only a moment after they'd walked out of the air-conditioned terminal into what felt like a solid wall of heat, the humidity making the air thick and sticky.

"And the sun is so bright," Heidi said.

Claudia laughed. "Yes, it's very different from home. It was three degrees when we left, and earlier this week, it snowed."

Izzy smiled. "I hope you didn't pack any jumpers because you won't be needing them."

Claudia shook her head, "But we did pack…what did you call them… togs?"

Izzy laughed. "Yes, togs. And those you will definitely need."

As they drove from the airport to the hotel, the children talked all the way, pointing out everything they saw and, after being patient at the airport, began asking Izzy lots of questions, mostly about things they could do while they were there. She was grateful for that because it meant she didn't have to come up with the conversation. She was also grateful that they didn't ask her any personal questions. Maybe Claudia had asked them not to. Whatever the reason, keeping the conversation light to start with was exactly what Izzy wanted. She wasn't ready to talk about anything personal yet. Not until she'd confirmed her first impression that things would be ok.

It didn't take them long to get to the front of the check-in queue, and Izzy waited in reception to ensure everything was okay. While Claudia and Andreas were filling out the forms, the children had their faces pressed against the glass wall that separated the reception area from the pool. No matter how much they asked, both Claudia and Andreas said they'd have to wait until tomorrow to go for a swim. It didn't help that the only people still in the pool at that time were children around the same age, jumping in from the edge, then swimming to the steps, getting out and jumping in again. Even though Izzy couldn't hear them, from the looks on their faces, she could tell they were shrieking with joy. The three children finally gave up asking, but only after they were promised that they could swim first thing in the morning. For people who'd spent a long time on a plane, they all seemed to have a lot of energy, but Andreas had said they'd all slept, something Izzy had never managed to do in the air. It was too hard to get comfortable enough to do so in those cramped seats. Although maybe their seats hadn't been cramped. Izzy hadn't asked, but she thought that they probably flew business class, something else she'd never managed to do. She could understand the children's energy, being in a new place, so different to anywhere they'd been before, so many new things to discover. Claudia, on the other hand, maybe hers was nervous energy. Izzy couldn't tell.

When check-in was complete, Claudia and her family headed to the elevators so they could go up to their room to shower and change. All the way across the lobby, the children talked excitedly about going in the pool the following morning. When the elevator doors shut, Izzy turned around and headed outside, deciding to go for a walk. She was glad she'd decided to dress for dinner so she didn't have to race home, change and come back. Izzy headed towards the City Botanic Gardens, thinking that a walk through the trees and along the river in the fading light of the day would calm her. The journey from the airport had been comfortable enough, thanks mainly to the children's conversation. But Claudia had hardly spoken, and she hadn't mentioned anything about their dad, so Izzy had been unable to pick up any clues as to how she was feeling about meeting him. She wished she'd picked up something so that if she needed to warn him, she could do so. But she had nothing. There was nothing she could do to make it easier for him. Still, she couldn't help but think again that things would be all right.

Izzy walked for forty-five minutes, sometimes taking in what was around her, occasionally stopping and wondering how she'd ended up where she was. When she did notice her surroundings, she also noticed the people, especially the families. Maybe she should have asked Trent to come early. She hadn't because she thought she'd want to be alone, but now that she was, Izzy began to think it was the wrong decision. As with earlier in the day, time went quickly, more quickly than Izzy was ready for.

     <u>The Diary and the Green Dress</u>

She took one last look at the river before leaving the peacefulness of the gardens and heading back into the hustle and bustle of the city. When she got to the hotel, she could see Trent standing outside.

"How do you feel?"

Izzy took a moment before she replied truthfully. "I don't know."

They stood outside, waiting in silence for Izzy's parents. No words came into Izzy's mind. She was glad Trent was holding her hand, though. When her parents arrived, she hugged them both. To anyone else, they looked fine, but Izzy could tell they were doing a good job of not showing their feelings. She leaned over and gave her mum another hug.

"I'll be all right," she said. "This is just not a situation I ever thought I would be faced with."

Her dad turned his head but not before Izzy saw the look of sadness on his face.

"We can wait a few minutes before we go in," Izzy said.

Julia shook her head. "We can't walk away now, so we may as well just do it."

"Are you sure?" Izzy said.

Julia nodded, and Ben took a step closer to her, grabbed hold of her hand and then nodded. Trent held the door open for them, and then he took hold of Izzy's hand. No one said anything as they walked over to the restaurant. Claudia and her family were already there, and she stood up when they reached the table.

"Hello," Claudia said.

"Hello," Ben replied.

Izzy watched as they looked at one another. They didn't hug or shake hands. They just kept looking at each other. Claudia broke the silence by introducing her family. Izzy's dad then introduced Julia and Trent. There were many hellos, but not much else was said until Trent suggested they sit down and ask for some menus. Izzy didn't think anyone was particularly hungry but perusing the menu and then ordering gave them something to do besides trying to think of what to say to each other. Izzy began to wonder if this was a bad idea and that maybe she and her dad should have met Claudia on her own and left the rest of the family out of it. From where she was sitting, she could see that her dad had reached across under the table and taken hold of her mum's hand again. He was the one who broke the silence.

"How was your flight?"

"It was good," Claudia said. "Very long, though."

Ben nodded. "It's a long way from Germany to here."

Neither of them said any more. It was Annamarie who broke the silence this time, completely unaware that's what she was doing.

"We've brought our swimmers. I can't wait to go to the beach. Mum said we can learn to surf."

Ben smiled. "That sounds like fun."

Heidi looked across the table at him. "You're our Opa, aren't you?"

"Yes, I am."

The children looked at each other, and then Rainer spoke up. "I'm very pleased to meet you."

Claudia laughed. "We all are."

Ever since they'd sat down, Izzy had been subtly looking from her dad to Claudia and back again. In the flesh, Izzy thought she might see more of Claudia's mum in her, but all Izzy could see was her dad, their dad, even down to the way Claudia rested her hands on the table while they were talking. Then there was the way she tilted her head slightly when she turned to look at someone. Claudia looked like the female version of him, even more so than Izzy did. And then there were Claudia's children. Heidi looked the most like her mum, Rainer the least. Annamarie was somewhere in the middle. But no one could look at any of them, even Rainer, and not think Ben was their grandfather.

"Can we have dessert?" Rainer asked.

     <u>The Diary and the Green Dress</u>

Andreas nodded. "Yes, it's been a long flight, so you deserve a treat."

"We don't have dessert very often," Heidi said.

Rainer nodded. "And it's not fair. I love dessert."

Claudia smiled. "I know you do, but it's not good for you. And you do get it occasionally."

"Not as much as I'd like."

Andreas leaned over and ruffled his hair. "You're allowed to have some now. What are you going to have?"

"I want to try this," Rainer said, pointing at something on the menu. "I've never heard of it before. I don't know how to say it either."

Ben looked at where he was pointing. "It's called pavlova."

"Is it yummy?" Rainer asked.

Ben smiled. "Yes, it is."

"Can I have one too?" Heidi asked.

"And me," Annamarie said.

Andreas nodded. "Yes, you can."

So three pavlovas were ordered. When they arrived, everyone else watched as they were devoured so quickly that all the pavlovas were gone long before anyone finished their coffee. They were mostly silent as they drank. Izzy noticed Claudia was looking at her dad, their dad, a lot.

"I might take my coffee and finish it by the window," Claudia said.

Ben looked at Julia and then Izzy before turning to Claudia. "I think I'll join you."

Izzy watched them as they stood by the window, wishing she could hear what they were saying, but there was no way without it looking obvious. And besides, she knew she shouldn't eavesdrop on a private conversation, no matter how tempting it was. While they were gone, the conversation at the table flowed more easily. The children talked about school and the things they liked to do when they weren't at school. All three were musical—Heidi played the piano, Rainer the guitar and Annamarie had just started learning the drums. Julia commented on their house being very noisy, and it was the first time Izzy saw her mum look directly at Claudia's family since they'd arrived.

Also, for the first time since they'd arrived, Julia asked a question. "How did you meet Claudia?"

"In our local bar. I was there with my friends one Sunday afternoon, and she was there with her friends. It was winter, and it had been raining all day, so the bar was more crowded than usual. We bumped into each other. Claudia's drink spilled, and I offered to buy her another one."

"It was meant to be."

"I think so. We've been together ever since. Meeting Claudia was the best thing to ever happen to me."

Heidi put her hands on her hips. "I thought we were the best thing to ever happen to you."

Andreas laughed. "You are as well, but if I hadn't met your mum, none of you would be here."

Heidi screwed her face up. "I don't want to know about that."

"About what?" Annamarie asked.

Andreas leaned over and hugged her. "Nothing for you to know about now. I'll tell you when you're a bit older."

"Izzy told me you're a high school science teacher."

"I enjoy it, although I don't think Heidi likes that her dad is a teacher at her school."

Heidi shook her head. "It's so embarrassing."

Children are the same the world over, Izzy thought to herself. She remembered all the times her dad had embarrassed her when she was Heidi's age. He'd been heavily involved in the P&C Committee, and all through grade eight, Izzy was constantly being called to the office to pick something up to take home to him. Now that she was an adult, she thought it was great that he'd been so involved. But at thirteen, every time she heard her name called over the PA system, she'd been mortified, the other kids looking at her thinking she was in trouble as she walked towards the office. It didn't take long before they realised why she went to the office so often, which was some consolation. She wondered if Claudia's German dad had embarrassed her when she was thirteen. She turned to look at her mum, thinking about what she'd been like back then and saw her looking over at the window. Andreas was looking in that direction too.

"Do you know why Claudia waited so long to contact us?" Izzy asked.

"She's talked about it ever since I've known her, but she never felt like it was the right time. And she was worried about hurting her stepdad's feelings."

"Is he upset that she wanted to meet her biological dad?" Izzy asked. "I thought he would have known that one day she'd want to."

"Yes, he knew but thinking it would happen and it actually happening are two different things. He raised Claudia as his own, and he loves her very much, so it's hard for him as well."

Izzy hadn't given any thought to how he would feel. She hadn't thought about how Claudia's mum would feel either.

"I'm glad mum finally thought it was the right time," Rainer said. "Because we're here now on this holiday, and we're going to the beach."

Everyone at the table laughed, and then the subject turned back to talking about their respective lives while they waited for the conversation at the window to end.

The next day, Teresa called to ask how it went, and Izzy spent an hour on the phone going over everything. She left out the conversation she'd had with her dad afterwards, the long phone call late at night after Trent was asleep. And after her mum had gone to sleep as well. She'd had enough to deal with already that day, and her dad didn't want to upset her anymore.

"It sounds like an emotional day."

Izzy sighed. "It was."

"Do you want me to come over?"

"You don't have to do that. Trent is here."

"That's okay. I'll come anyway."

Izzy laughed. "You just want to read the last of the diary entries."

"I'm thinking of you. It will take your mind off things. And so will the bottle of wine that I bring."

Half an hour later, Teresa was sitting in Izzy's lounge room while Trent filled three glasses. Izzy pulled the pages from the envelope.

16 May 1968

A lot of memories with Bryce have come flooding back. Like the first time we had a picnic together. Back then, our picnic spot was just an open field by a creek, and people rarely went there. It was too far out of town. That's why we chose it. Now our picnic spot has tables, chairs, BBQs and swings. The first time he took me there, it was a beautiful, warm, sunny day, and there was no one in sight. Bryce took a blanket out of the car and spread it out along the bank. I had prepared a picnic, and Bryce had brought a bottle of wine. I had only ever had a couple of glasses of wine before then, or any other alcohol for that matter, but sitting by the river, sipping the wine, watching the water flow slowly by and the feel of the sun on my skin—it was perfect. And later in the afternoon, when we made love on the blanket, it was nothing like it was with Martin, and I remember thinking that this must be how it's supposed to be. We had three more picnics there before I realised I was pregnant with Hettie.

24 May 1968

I saw Bryce again today. He took me out for lunch. He joked about having a picnic, but neither of us wants to sit on the ground anymore. It's too uncomfortable and too hard to get back up, so we just went to the café near my house. They know me there, and the food is good. Our waitress asked about Bryce, and I said he was an old friend. She replied that it was

     The Diary and the Green Dress

nice to have people in your life that you'd known for a long time. I agreed but didn't say any more. It's no one else's business, and it's a complicated story. Bryce and I talked for two hours, and we kept our conversation to what had happened in our lives since we'd last seen each other. I don't think either of us is ready to talk about the time before he went away.

30 May 1968

Hettie arrived earlier today than she said she would. Bryce was just walking down the front stairs as she came through the gate. I introduced him as a friend that I hadn't seen in a very long time. She asked him if he'd known Martin, and he told her he used to work for the family. They looked at each other for a few moments before Hettie said, nice to meet you and then walked into the house.

12 June 1968

Hettie saw Bryce and me having coffee this morning and called this afternoon to say she'd like to talk to him. I think she wants to ask about Martin. When Hettie was young, she and Martin weren't close, but when she became an adult, she was closer to him than she was with me. When Martin started getting better, he became very protective of her, even though she was taking care of herself by then. They spent a lot of time together, more than most fathers and daughters did at the time. I was happy about it because it was helping Martin with his recovery, something that had been a very long time coming, and Hettie seemed content when she was with him. In truth, I held back a little with Hettie when she was growing up. The grief I felt because of Lily was so deep and all-consuming. I was scared that if something happened to her like it did to Lily, I'd never recover. And now she's going to meet Bryce tomorrow.

13 June 1968

I'm tired, and Hettie suspects something. She didn't say anything, but I know she does. We met for lunch, Hettie, Bryce and me. I thought lunch was better than tea or coffee because you can't talk as much when you're eating. I was careful about what I said, and so was Bryce. Hettie was interested to know if we knew each other outside of Bryce working for my father. He told her that he helped me with things that needed to be done at the house while Martin was away. Hettie knows that Martin needed some help after he came back from the war. I've told her some of the details but not everything. Martin wouldn't have wanted that. Bryce didn't go into any details either, and I was grateful. Hettie asked what sort of things he did to help, and Bryce told her how he fixed anything that was broken and that he'd drive me where I needed to go. Hettie is still amazed that I've never learnt to drive. I remember how much I wanted to learn, but neither Martin nor Father would let me. Such an archaic notion now – let me. But that's what it was like back then. Hettie got her licence as soon as she could. She doesn't like to rely on anyone for anything, and there was no one to stop her. She also wanted to know about my parents. She knew them as a child, and I have spoken about them over the years, but Bryce knew them differently, and that's what she was interested in. We spent about an hour and a half at lunch. Hettie and Bryce got on very well. They have similar personalities. Hettie didn't say much on the way home. After talking a lot over lunch, she was very quiet in the car.

24 June 1968

Bryce and I went to an art gallery today. Hanging on one of the walls was a painting of Alexander's. It's been a long time since I've seen one, and I'd forgotten how good they are. Bryce didn't say anything at first. He just stood and stared. Eventually, he smiled. I know how much he would have liked to see his brother before he died, but there had been very little contact after Alexander left. He never came back to Brisbane, and Bryce never had the money to travel to France. Neither of them were great letter writers either. I only know of one letter Bryce wrote, and it wasn't to Alexander. Before he died, though, Alexander sent him two paintings. They were paintings that he'd done especially for Bryce. The first was of the farm where they grew up. The second was of the two brothers when they were teenagers. Bryce has hung them in the front room of his house, so you see them as soon as you walk in. They're both beautiful, and I always pause for a moment to look at them before I step any further inside.

26 June 1968

I've been thinking about the night Bryce stayed. We never should have done that. It was far too dangerous. I can't believe no one found out. Or maybe they did and never said anything. Either way, it was a considerable risk to take. I still remember how wonderful it felt waking up

     The Diary and the Green Dress

next to him. We'd stayed up until the early hours of the morning talking. It was the first time he'd told me about his family in detail. I could fill pages with what he said, but I won't. I'll just say I'm glad he had to stay and help with the farm instead of going to war. I'm so happy that he had a falling out with his father over how the farm should be run, leaving afterwards and choosing a life in the city. If not, I never would have met him. I never understood why Alexander went back to France, the country of his pain and sorrow, the country that filled his nightmares. Do we ever really understand the choices we make?

"Well, that solves that mystery of why Bryce didn't go to war," Izzy said. "And there's a photo stuck to the back of this page."

Grace was in the middle wearing the green dress. On her left was Martin in a suit. On her right, also in a suit, was Bryce.

"It could have been taken before they started their affair," Trent said.

Teresa shook her head. "Bryce is standing as close to Grace as Martin is. I don't think they'd be standing that close if Grace only knew him as the manager at her dad's factory."

"You're right," Izzy said. "I wonder if anyone else picked up on that."

"Do you think people picked up on that sort of thing back then?" Trent asked.

Teresa nodded. "Of course they did. They just didn't talk about it as openly as we do now."

Izzy looked down at the photo again. What had been going through Grace's mind as she stood between Martin and Bryce? Had Jason ever stood between Izzy and one of the women he was having an affair with? And if he had, what had gone through his mind?

Chapter Twenty One

The dress looked so beautiful, almost too beautiful to wear. Katherine had done a fantastic job repairing it. She'd also added a layer underneath to give the original material something to attach to and make it stronger. Izzy didn't know where they were going for dinner because Trent said it was a surprise. He did tell her to dress up, though, and she couldn't think of a better dress to wear. She ran her fingers along the material one more time before slipping it over her head and turning to face the mirror. It fit her so well it was like it had been made especially for her. She took one last look in the mirror, picked up the matching clutch purse and headed out to the verandah where Trent was waiting.

"You look amazing," Trent said. "That dress is perfect on you."

Izzy looked around and saw that Trent had lit some candles, and there was a bottle of champagne chilling in an ice bucket.

"I thought we could have a drink before we go. We've got plenty of time before we need to be at the restaurant."

"That sounds nice. The candlelight is beautiful too."

"It's our first anniversary so I thought I should do something special. And these are for you."

Trent pulled out a bunch of apricot roses, her favourite, from behind the chair where he'd hidden them.

Izzy looked down at the biggest bunch of roses she'd ever received. "They're beautiful. Thank you. But I thought we agreed we weren't going to get each other anything."

"I know, but I saw the flowers, and I had to get them."

Izzy hugged him. "I'm feeling very spoilt."

Trent smiled. "Good, because you deserve to be."

They sat on the verandah and talked and looked at the stars until Trent said it was time to go. He finally told her that he'd booked a table at The Summit restaurant located on Mt Coot-tha. Neither of them had been there before, and Trent had said he thought it would be a good place for an anniversary dinner. When they got there, she saw he was right. The view was amazing, looking down at the lights of Brisbane. Trent had booked the table right next to the glass wall, so they had an uninterrupted view while they ate. As Izzy looked at the view, she thought about everything that had happened since she'd met Trent just prior to Christmas the year before. If someone had told her what the following twelve months would bring, she wouldn't have believed them. Settling into a recently purchased house wasn't out of the ordinary. Neither was being in a relationship. But Claudia, that was something she never would have predicted. She wondered what Claudia and her family were doing that night. They'd seen each other twice more since the dinner, the first time at the hotel where the children spent the whole time in the pool. And the second was when they walked through the city looking at the Christmas decorations before hopping onto a City Cat and cruising up the river. Having something to do helped take the pressure off making conversation even though both times, Izzy was surprised at how soon the conversation started to flow. And both times, her mum seemed more relaxed around Claudia and her family. And her dad looked happy, not every minute though, as Izzy caught the occasional glimpse of sadness on his face. Claudia was in his life now, but it would take a long time to be at peace with the forty-two years he didn't know about.

By the time she'd finished eating what she'd ordered, Izzy was so full that she didn't even want to look at the dessert menu. Trent did, though.

"Let's just share one. The first two courses were so good, we should at least try something."

"I don't know if I can. The entrée and main were much bigger than I thought they'd be."

"I'm sure you can manage one bite."

She looked at him as he read the dessert menu. He'd gone to so much trouble to make this a nice night for her that she figured one tiny bite wouldn't hurt.

"Okay, you've talked me into it."

Izzy let Trent pick something, and when it came out, the waiter placed it in front of Izzy. She was just about to put the spoon into the bowl when she looked down and saw a diamond ring. She stared at it for a few moments, realising that the ring was too beautiful and too big for it to be just an anniversary ring.

"I guess you realise what I'm going to say next," Trent said.

Izzy couldn't find any words, so she just nodded.

"I've never been happier, and I want to spend the rest of my life with you. Will you marry me?"

Izzy hadn't been expecting a proposal, but she said the only thing that made sense to her. "Yes."

Trent smiled, picked up the ring and slid it on her finger.

"It's beautiful," Izzy said. "You picked well".

"I can't take all the credit. I had some help."

Izzy smiled. "Let me guess…Teresa?"

Trent nodded. "She was very excited."

"I'm sure she was."

Izzy could picture Teresa taking Trent from store to store until she'd found the ring that was now on Izzy's finger.

"How long did she have to keep the secret for?"

"I've had the ring for the past three weeks."

Izzy had seen Teresa twice during that time, and she couldn't think of anything she'd said or done that would have given Izzy a hint. Teresa had kept the secret well. Maybe she'd been right when she said that one day Izzy would have a photo like the one she'd seen of Claudia and her

     The Diary and the Green Dress

family before they arrived.

"Merry Christmas."

Izzy opened her eyes and saw Trent standing there with a breakfast tray. He'd cooked bacon and eggs and poured two glasses of champagne and orange juice.

Izzy smiled as she wiped the sleep from her eyes. "That looks amazing. I can't believe you got up without waking me and did all of this."

"It's our first Christmas living together. And our first one engaged. So I thought we should start the day the right way."

After breakfast and still in their pyjamas, they sat down on the lounge room floor next to the Christmas tree to exchange gifts. When all the presents that Izzy could see were opened, Trent reached to the back of the tree and pulled out a small box with a bow on top.

"I hope you like it."

The wrapping was done so beautifully that Izzy knew it had been done in a store. She slowly undid the wrapping. She lifted the lid and saw diamonds glistening on top of a small cushion—earrings that were the matching set to her engagement ring. Izzy gasped. They were beautiful.

"I don't think like is the right word. I love them."

She leaned over and kissed him. For the second time that morning, she felt grateful for everything, and everyone, she had in her life.

"Come on, we better get ready, or we'll be late getting to your parents' house."

While Trent put the presents, for her now extended family, in the car, Izzy wandered from room to room wondering what Grace had done after waking on what should have been Lily's second Christmas morning. How did she get out of bed and make it through the day? Two Christmas mornings, so many years apart, Izzy's filled with happiness and Grace's filled with sadness.

All the way to her parents, she kept thinking of Grace, Lily, Hettie,

Bryce, and Martin. And she realised that all of them had lives full of pain, even Lily, who was so young but had died in pain and probably frightened, not old enough to know what was happening. Izzy may have had some ups and downs, but nothing compared to what they all went through, and she realised she was much luckier than she'd ever thought.

Izzy took one last look at the table. She and Trent had arrived early to help her parents get ready for Christmas lunch. Every place setting had plates, cutlery, glasses, napkins and of course, bonbons. In the middle of the table was a red and green wreath surrounding a collection of gold candles. Every time she'd put a bonbon in place, she'd glanced down at the diamond on her finger, still not used to it.

She walked over to the tree covered in decorations and blinking lights. Ever since she was a child, it was Izzy's job to put the angel on top, and she'd come over on the first of December to do just that. The difference this year, under the tree, there were presents for Claudia and her family. "The table looks beautiful, Izzy," her mum said as she walked into the room.

"Thanks. The smells coming from the kitchen are amazing."

"I can only take credit for some of that. Trent is an amazing cook."

Izzy nodded then patted her stomach. "And if he keeps cooking the way he does, I won't be able to fit into my clothes."

"Are Claudia and her family still coming at 11.30 am?"

Izzy nodded. "That will give us time to open presents before lunch."

Izzy's mum looked at the presents under the tree and then back at the table.

Izzy reached over and held her hand. "Are you still okay with them coming to Christmas lunch?"

Izzy's mum didn't say anything for a few moments.

"If I had a choice, I'd rather none of this had happened. I spent so long trying for a second child."

Her mum turned away and waited a minute before continuing.

"But I can't change the past, and Claudia and her family are part of our family now. It will get easier over time."

At precisely 11.30 am, the doorbell rang. When Izzy opened the door, she was greeted with the sight of Claudia and her family, arms laden with presents, each of them in Christmas attire. Claudia and her daughters wore dresses made from material with miniature Christmas trees all over it, while Andreas and Rainer were wearing red pants and green t-shirts with Santa Claus on them. Claudia laughed when she saw Izzy looking at what they were wearing.

"We dress like this every year. Although this year, we didn't need to bring the matching jumpers and coats."

"Come in," Izzy said. "The tree is over there if you want to put the presents under it."

Izzy watched as they walked over to the tree, talking to each other in German, and she wondered what they were saying. She'd always said she should learn another language. Now she had a reason to do it. Maybe Claudia could teach her.

"Let's go out to the verandah," Izzy said. "There's some pre-lunch nibbles and drinks."

Izzy's parents and Trent were already out there, and Claudia laughed when she saw how they were looking at her family. "Izzy had the same look on her face when she saw us. It's our Christmas tradition."

"You look very festive," Julia said.

Ben walked over to the table. "Can I get you all a drink? Champagne for the adults and punch for the children."

Izzy watched him as he poured the drinks. He looked more relaxed and more at peace now that he and Claudia had spent some time together, just the two of them. Claudia also looked relaxed. And very happy. Her children kept looking around and staring out at the view.

"This is their first Christmas where it hasn't been cold," Claudia said.

"At home, we stay inside."

"And sometimes it snows," Rainer said.

Julia smiled at him. "I've never had a white Christmas."

"You can visit us now," Andreas said.

Claudia nodded. "We have a lovely cabin in a forest that we go to, and it always snows there."

A cabin in the middle of snow-covered woods. Even her mum would enjoy that, Izzy thought to herself. Maybe they would go. Maybe next year.

"I suppose there are a lot of things that are different from what we do at Christmas," Izzy said.

Claudia nodded. "We eat hot foods because of the weather. We always have duck and potato dumplings, and each year we alternate between goose and rabbit."

"I've never tried rabbit," Julia said.

"It's very nice," Claudia said. "And in the past few years, we've had salmon as well."

"We're having salmon today," Julia said. "But it's smoked salmon, and it's cold."

Annamarie piped up. "I love smoked salmon."

Julia smiled again. "It's a good thing I bought plenty then."

Heidi turned around and pointed at the tree. "That's different to what we have too. We always have a real tree."

"A real tree wouldn't last long in this heat," Ben said. "So we use that one every year."

Heidi thought about it for a minute. "That makes sense, I suppose. Do you have Christmas markets? I love going to Christmas markets."

Heidi told them about the markets near their home with the stalls with handcrafted items, the decorations and the lights and the nativity scene in the middle of the markets.

 The Diary and the Green Dress

"And Mama and Papa always have mulled wine."

Andreas smiled. "Just to keep warm."

Ben smiled too. "That's what I say about a cold beer on a hot summer's day, except that it's to keep cool, not warm."

They stood on the verandah for a while longer, talking and sipping their champagne and punch before the children got impatient for the presents.

"They've done well waiting this long," Julia said. "Let's go inside."

Izzy watched as the children unwrapped their gifts. It was lovely to see the joy on their faces.

"Look what we've got," Heidi said, holding up her present. "Thank you!"

Annamarie and Rainer nodded and said thank you in unison as they also held up the confirmation paper for their surf lessons.

Claudia smiled. "That was very thoughtful of you all."

"I can't wait," Rainer said.

Annamarie nodded. "It's going to be so much fun."

They opened the rest of their presents—things that Claudia and Andreas had brought from Germany for Izzy and her family. Things with an Australian theme were given to Claudia and Andreas. Izzy's dad had watched Claudia and her family open their presents closely as if he was thinking about all the other Christmases he had missed. Izzy thought back to the conversation they'd had late on the night after he first met Claudia in person. They'd talked for an hour about everything that had happened prior to the dinner and the conversation he and Claudia had by the window. She never felt upset that he hadn't tried to contact her. Her mum had explained the situation, and while she'd always been happy with the explanation, she hadn't given a lot of thought to the fact that he didn't know she existed. And when she had started to think about it, that was when she realised she wanted to meet him one day. She wasn't expecting them to act like family straight away, but even though it was their first face-to-face meeting, she could tell already that would come. When her dad began to speak, Claudia listened, and for the first time, began to doubt that her mum had done the right thing in not trying to contact him in later years when it became easier to connect with people no matter where they were in the world. The past couldn't be changed, though. But they could change the present and the future, and that's what they agreed to do.

Lunch lasted longer than Izzy thought it would. No one seemed in a hurry to stop eating, especially the children, or to leave the table. When Claudia complimented Izzy's mum on the food, she smiled. She smiled again when Claudia thanked her for going to so much trouble to make them feel welcome and including them on Christmas Day. After they left, laden with presents, and after they'd all pitched in to clean up, Izzy realised it was one of the best Christmas Days she'd ever had.

When she and Trent finally got home that night, they were both tired. But there were still some pages in the envelope they hadn't read. Even though the day had gone better than Izzy could ever have wished for, and as much as she'd enjoyed herself, she wanted a break from thinking about her now extended family.

Dear Grace

I don't feel comfortable writing things down, but I'm less comfortable talking about them. The first few sessions with the doctor weren't successful because I didn't say much. At the end of the third session, the doctor asked me to write letters. Instead of talking in person, he wants me to talk via words on a page. I've decided to address the letters to you because it's easier to write when I think of it as an actual letter. You'll never get the letters, though. You've had enough to deal with. When I think about how much you've suffered because of Lily, it almost destroys me. I can't fix it, and I don't want to add to it, which is why I will not give you these. I think of Lily every day, as I know you do. I don't say it, though. She was so small, so fragile. It was my job to protect her, and I didn't. You must hate me for that.

Martin

    <u>The Diary and the Green Dress</u>

Dear Grace

It was never a thought I wouldn't go. It was expected. I heard later that some of the men who didn't go were handed white feathers, which made me angry. They weren't cowards. They were strong for standing up for what they believed in. I think they were the lucky ones. There were a few of us who signed up together. We'd known each other since we were children. We grew up together, went to school together, knew each other's families. We were going overseas to do our part for King and Country. That's how we referred to it—going overseas. It would be over by Christmas, we said. Of course, it wasn't, and I was there until the end. At first, I was terrified every single moment. Not that I let anyone see. The first time I saw someone die, I didn't have time to think about it because I was running. It's hard to run in mud when you're carrying a rifle. It was only when I got out of the mud and back into the trench that I realised it wasn't just one person who died but many. I huddled against the trench wall, and I'm ashamed to say I vomited. I'm also ashamed to say that after a while, it didn't bother me anymore. I became numb and blocked things out. I had to. I wouldn't have survived otherwise. I never thought I would shoot another human being, but I quickly realised if I didn't, they would shoot me. It shocked me how quickly I started firing back. During my training, there was a sergeant who'd been in the army for a long time and who'd fought in battle. He told us to practice firing as much as possible so that we would do it without thinking when we went into battle. It turned out he was right. Even amid guns, grenades and death, I picked up my rifle and pulled the trigger over and over again. I've never thought about how many people I've killed. How many families have lived with years of grieving for a son, a brother, a husband who died because of me? If I thought about it, I would lose my mind. I'm halfway there now. Isn't that why I'm here? The doctors say it's shell shock, but it must be more than that. I feel so old, as if my life is already over.

Martin

Dear Grace

I wrote two types of letters during the war—the letters addressed to you, but never sent, and the letters to the families of the men who died. The letters to you, how could I burden you with knowledge of the never-ending mud, lice and rats, about the empty farmhouses that had rooms missing because of the shelling, about the shops that had no food for sale. And the towns we went back to with fewer soldiers than before and how the locals grieved for those men too. Friendships had formed in those towns and sometimes more than friendships.

Writing the other letters was hard, but I had to send those. The official notification is so cold, and I thought the families deserved something more. But how do you write to a mother who will never see her 19-year-old son again? Or to a 27-year-old wife and tell her that her husband will not return, and her children will grow up without a father? I often thought about how many of our generation would be left by the end. The day I had to write to William Thomas' parents, I kept picturing Billy and me when we were ten walking down to the creek and skipping stones on the water. Then there was the day I had to write to Andrew Marshall's wife, and I remembered their wedding day. She was pregnant when we left. They'd only been married six months when we shipped out.

When I came back, people congratulated me on what a fine job I did. But in the back of their minds, I knew they thought why him and why not our loved one? I ask myself that question often. Why did I survive when so many didn't?

Martin

Dear Grace

This is the fourth and final letter that I have been told to write. The doctors have said more than once that they won't read them unless I allow them to. I don't know about that. I understand that if I show them, it may help in a quicker recovery, but for now, I still need to think that no one will read them, or I won't write. One of my doctors has asked me to focus on Lily this time, so I will try. But it's hard to write about Lily. I loved her from the first moment I saw her. Before that moment, I didn't realise you could love someone so completely in an instant. Holding her for the first time was wonderful, and from that moment, I knew I had to do everything I could to protect her. But I failed.

I also wish I could have been there for you, but I was too caught up in my own grief. When I came back, I was distant, and that hasn't changed. You always ask me what's wrong and if you can help, but there is nothing you can do. After all the horrors that I lived through, you and Lily were the reminders of what could be good in the world. And then Lily was taken away.

Martin

Izzy carefully folded Martin's letters back up and placed them in the envelope, glad she'd read them and had a better idea of who he was and how he'd felt. But she felt sad too. After everything he'd seen and done, he was expected to come home and act like nothing had happened. There was no one for him to talk to, nowhere to get help before it was too late and he was taken away. Grace had needed support back then, and so had he. But neither of them received it.

There was only one page left they hadn't read, and Izzy waited for a moment before unfolding it, thinking about Martin and how she now knew he was different from how Grace had portrayed him. Not surprisingly though as he was unable to say anything, and all she could go on was what she could see in front of her. When she unfolded it, she saw that it started with a date.

I've read all of Martin's letters now, the ones I have just found hidden in the inside pocket of his army jacket and the one I found years ago. I felt sad when I read them, this last one in particular because he talked about Lily. I didn't cry, though. I used up my allowance of tears many years ago. At the time, I didn't know it was possible to cry so much. I never thought the tears would end. I still feel sad every time I think of her, but I no longer cry. For all those years, we could have comforted each other instead of dealing with our grief alone. But I never knew Martin felt like he did. I'm glad he didn't throw out the letters. If he had, I never would have known. I've been thinking since I read them, would I have still fallen in love with Bryce if Martin had been able to talk to me, been able to let me help him? Or if he had been there for me like I needed?

Chapter Twenty Two

The alarm went off earlier than she would have liked, but she got up anyway, having already told Claudia and her family she would drive them to the Gold Coast. They couldn't check in until 2 pm, but that wasn't of any concern to Heidi, Rainer and Annamarie. They'd waited long enough to swim in the ocean, and they weren't going to wait a moment longer. With her car already full, Trent would follow in his car with her parents. She had no idea how they had managed to book an apartment at the last minute in the same complex as Claudia and her family over the Christmas holidays. Apartments on the Gold Coast with an ocean view booked out months in advance. But when she and Trent had looked, there was one two-bedroom apartment available, the only one in the part of the coast where Claudia had booked.

Izzy yawned as she got in the car, wishing last night's dinner hadn't gone so late. But there was no way Teresa would let Claudia out of the country without meeting her, so Izzy had organised a dinner. Teresa and Claudia didn't stop talking all night. It was only when Izzy reminded Claudia about the early start the following morning that they said good night after swapping phone numbers and email addresses. And after Claudia had told Teresa that she and her family were welcome to visit them anytime. From how they got on, if Izzy didn't hurry up and make plans, Teresa would get to Germany before she did.

"Look at the waves," Rainer said. "I can't wait to go in."

All three children tumbled out of the car and then stood still, mesmerized by the ocean. The water was bright blue in the sunshine, and the waves were rolling in one long continuous swell of water, not a choppy wave in sight.

"Who are they?" Annamarie said, pointing towards a man and woman in the familiar yellow and red shirts.

"They're lifesavers," Ben said.

"What's a lifesaver?"

"Some people aren't strong swimmers, and sometimes the water is rough, so if anyone gets into trouble, they help you out of the water."

Rainer looked at them and then turned to look at his grandfather. "We won't get into any trouble. We're all good swimmers. And mum made us practice in the pool near us before we left."

Ben smiled. "You'll be fine then."

Izzy looked at the water and then back at the children. Swimming in a pool was much different to swimming in the ocean. But it was a calm day, and there were no warning signs up, so she figured they'd be fine. Besides, the water was already full of swimmers, many of them small children, and they were all having a ball.

"Can I put my thongs on now?" Rainer said.

Everyone laughed as he said it. He'd been practising how to say the word thongs since Ben had bought all three children a pair. None of the shoes they brought with them were suitable for the beach.

"Yes, you should put them on now. But make sure you keep them on when you walk onto the beach. The sand will be hot."

Rainer looked at his grandfather and then at the people on the beach down near the water's edge, most of whom were barefoot. He walked to the start of the path to the beach with his thongs on but took them off once he was on the sand. He only lasted a few moments.

"My feet are burning!"

"I told you to leave them on. Wait until you get to the harder sand down near the water, and then take them off."

Claudia and Andreas hadn't even finished taking their new beach towels out of their bags before the children ran into the water. Izzy and Trent followed them in, giving the others a chance to get set up on the beach. The children amused themselves, ducking under and diving over the waves,

     The Diary and the Green Dress

until they saw the surfers over to their left. They were mesmerised by the way they rode the waves all the way into the shore.

"That will be us soon," Heidi said.

Izzy smiled. "They've probably been doing that for a long time. Maybe to start with, you should just concentrate on standing up."

Heidi thought about it for a minute and then agreed.

By the time 2 pm arrived, the children had been in the water for hours and showed no signs of getting out. It took several requests before they got out, all of them with a sad look on their faces. The only thing that finally worked was the promise they could go swimming again once they'd settled into their room.

When they arrived at the apartments they were staying in, Izzy stood and stared, thinking there was something familiar about them but not realising at first what it was. Then it dawned on her. It was the same apartment block she'd stayed in with her parents when she was twelve. The same one she'd seen in the photos she'd looked at not that long ago. Photos taken when there was only three of them. It looked different now, modernised with a restaurant on the ground floor and a bar overlooking the beach. When she'd booked their room online, it hadn't registered at all that it was the same place.

"Thank you for driving us, Izzy," Claudia said.

"That's ok. I hope you enjoy your holiday."

"We'll enjoy it more now that you're all staying for the next two days."

Izzy helped them carry their bags up, and once everything was inside, she went out to the balcony to look at the view. It was just as she remembered. Claudia came to stand beside her.

"It's a beautiful view," Claudia said.

"There's something calming about looking at the ocean."

"Yes, I thought that might be something I would need, but it turns out I don't. I wasn't sure what would happen when I got here."

Izzy turned to look at her. "I wasn't sure either."

"I'm glad we've had this time together."

"Me too."

"I grew up without a sister, so it's nice to know I have one now."

They were interrupted by a knock on the door.

"Great unit," Trent said as he walked in, Izzy's parents just behind. "Good choice Claudia."

"I found it online, and it had lots of great reviews. Plus, I like the idea of walking out the front of the building and straight onto the sand."

Izzy watched as her parents looked around.

"There's something familiar about this place," Ben said.

Izzy put her arm around him. "I'll tell you why later. Right now, I think we should get a photo."

Andreas gathered the children, who had no interest in being in a photo, not when the ocean was still calling them. But they came under protest and stood with Izzy, Trent, Ben, Julia, Claudia and Andreas. Then, with the ocean in the background, Izzy set up her camera to take a photo of all of them, her extended family. It would never replace the photo taken of just the three of them when she was twelve. But she would make room in her photo album to place this new one beside it.

Shelley Banks is a passionate writer who enjoys creating a story that will entertain readers. She is the author of *One Weekend,* a full-length novel that poses the question…How well do you really know those close to you? *Short, Sweet and September*, her second book, is a mix of fiction and non-fiction short reads, perfect for when you're short on time.

She is also the author of September Sprouts (septembersprouts.wordpress.com), a fiction and non-fiction blog that aims to encourage people to read.

Shelley lives in Gordon Park, Queensland, Australia. You can contact Shelley via:

Facebook https://www.facebook.com/writershellb/
Instagram https://www.instagram.com/writershellb/